WET DREAMS ON LOCKDOWN

The Librarian

ASHLEY WILLIAMS

URBAN AINT DEAD

URBAN AINT DEAD PRESENTS

Wet Dreams On Lockdown:
The Librarian

By Ashley Williams

URBAN AINT DEAD

P.O Box 448
Maybrook, NY 12543

Contact Author on FB: Authoress Ashley Williams / IG: @authoress_ashley_williams

Contact Publisher at www.urbanaintdead.com

Email: urbanaintdead@gmail.com

ISBN: 979-8-9902387-1-8

CONTENTS

SOUNDTRACKS

Scan the QR Code below to listen to the Soundtracks/Singles of some of your favorite U.A.D titles:

Don't have Spotify or Apple Music?
No Sweat!
Visit your choice streaming platform and search URBAN AINT DEAD.

Currently on lock serving a bid?
JPay, iHeartRadio, WHATEVER!
We got you covered.

Simply log into your facility's kiosk or tablet, go to music and search URBAN AINT DEAD.

URBAN AINT DEAD

Like & Follow us on social media:

FB - URBAN AINT DEAD

IG: @urbanaintdead

Tik Tok - @urbanaintdead

SUBMISSIONS

Submit the first three chapters of your completed manuscript to urbanaintdead@gmail.com, subject line: Your book's title. The manuscript must be in a .doc file and sent as an attachment. The document should be in Times New Roman, double-spaced, and in size 12 font. Also, provide your synopsis and full contact information. If sending multiple submissions, they must each be in a separate email. Have a story but no way to submit it electronically? You can still submit to URBAN AINT DEAD. Send in the first three chapters, written or typed, of your completed manuscript to:

URBAN AINT DEAD
P.O Box 448
Maybrook, NY 12543

DO NOT send original manuscript. Must be a duplicate.
Provide your synopsis and a cover letter containing your full
contact information.
Thanks for considering URBAN AINT DEAD.

nigga was tired of the same shit on a day-to-day basis, but hell, what could I expect? For the last 15 years, a nigga was the property of the Mississippi Department of Corrections, known as inmate #0654321. Yep, I went from being a free man to property of this fucked up state, all because I let my temper get the best of me.

I was caught on my charge of manslaughter on March 4th, 2008. A nigga was only 25 at the time, and I was in the streets heavy as fuck. Back then, there wasn't shit nobody could tell me because a nigga head was hard as fuck. My people always used to say to me that I didn't believe pig pussy was pork. Truth was, I didn't. Out in the streets, I didn't feel like nobody was fucking with me when it came to money, cars, and, of course, bitches. I had it all, and in the blink of an eye, that shit was all gone.

On March 4th, I kicked it out West in the projects. I didn't come out here often because these niggas out this way didn't fuck with us South Side niggas. The only reason I was even out this way was because of a little bitch that wanted to be on my team. She had been hitting a nigga up all day, begging me to come drop some dick off in her. Since I didn't have shit else to do that night, I decided to go ahead and stop by.

When I pulled up, I saw a few niggas standing outside, trying to see who the fuck was pulling up in the all-black Crown Victoria. Parking, I pulled out my phone and texted the old girl to let her know I was there. She responded and let me know to come inside the apartment.

Before leaving the car, I checked my surroundings to ensure I was good. Even though I felt like I was that nigga, I wasn't trying to take any chances and get caught slacking. With my gun in my waist, I got out of the car and made my way into the apartment.

As she said, I noticed it was slightly open when I reached the door. Entering the apartment, I instantly felt like something was off. For one, it was dark as fuck, and I also noticed that it was empty as fuck. Everything in me told me to turn around and get on down, but my tuff ass decided to stay.

I called out to ole girl to see if she was in the apartment, but I didn't get anything but silence in return.

I felt like something was about to pop off. I turned around

and was about to exit the apartment. As I reached for the door handle, I felt a gun being pressed against the back of my head.

What the fuck? I thought to myself. *Ain't no way I let a bitch set me up.*

"Mane, you know what it is," the nigga holding the gun stated.

"Bruh, you're wasting your time with this one. I ain't got shit on me," I let him know.

"You a fucken lie. My homegirl said you were that nigga out South, and I know y'all boys got plenty of money!" the nigga barked, never taking the gun off the back of my head.

I couldn't lie, a nigga was scared as hell. My whole life flashed before my eyes, but I refused to go out like a little bitch behind some pussy.

After going back and forth with the nigga, he dropped the gun and told me to get the fuck out before he changed his mind and shot my ass anyway.

Not wanting to give the nigga a chance to change his mind, I opened the door and took off in a full sprint towards my car.

As soon as I made it to my car, I cranked it up and put that bitch in reverse. I was both pissed off and relieved at the same time. I was pissed because this hoe-ass bitch had set a nigga up, and I was relieved because the nigga let me go with my life.

"If I ever see that hoe again, Imma kill that bitch," I said as

I hit the steering wheel, making my way out of the apartment complex.

Before I could make it entirely out, I spotted the bitch that set me up. Without thinking, I put the car in park, jumped out, and ran down on her ass. At that point, I didn't give a fuck that she was out there with her people. I just had to let this bitch know that she had fucked with the wrong one.

"Say bitch, you thought you were gonna set a real nigga up, huh!" I shouted as soon as I got in her personal space. The bitch couldn't say shit because she knew she had fucked up.

Not giving her time to answer me, I reached into my waistband, took my gun out, and instantly shot her in her muthafucken head, then turned around and made it back to my car. I had to get the fuck up out of there because I did that shit out in the open.

I was still pissed, but I felt better that I took care of that hoe. *I bet that bitch won't set anybody else up again*; I thought as I continued to make my way home.

Just thinking about that night made me wish to go back in time and change my actions, but here I was, out of sight and out of mind. I used to spend my days running wild, and now my every move was clocked, and I spent my days going through a fucken routine.

My day began at the crack of dawn when the guards would come through and make us all get up and get ready to go and eat. Before leaving my bed, I would lie there for a few minutes and reflect on the life I had left behind; for some reason, every day for the last 15 years, that was always my first thought of the day.

Breakfast in the prison cafeteria was a hurried affair. We had to be in and out within 20-25 minutes. The meals were bland, often watery oatmeal or gritty scrambled eggs. As always, I would scarf down my food, all while exchanging nods with my fellow inmates, acknowledging the unspoken camaraderie that had developed among us.

After breakfast, those who had jobs headed off to our work assignment. I was part of a small crew responsible for maintaining the prison grounds. Under the watchful eyes of the guards, we mowed lawns, trimmed hedges, and picked litter. It was grueling work for no pay, but it gave me a sense of purpose and a brief escape from the confines of my cell.

Since we kept things up daily, we were done with our assignments by the time we were set to go to lunch. Lunchtime offered a brief respite from the day's monotony. I usually would sit with a small group of friends, sharing stories and cracking jokes to forget our grim reality momentarily. Also, while in the prison cafeteria, some inmates would trade goods – cigarettes, snacks, or contraband items discreetly passed from one hand to another. I tended to stay away from that. I didn't have the time to owe anybody anything, and I also refused to go through the hassle of getting into it with anybody for owing me something.

In the afternoon, we were granted a few hours of recreation time. We could play basketball, lift weights, or walk around the fenced-in yard. This was one of these moments of physical activity essential for maintaining my sanity and fitness. Working out kept me looking good and helped me release stress if I had anything going on.

I liked to go to the library and chill out for a little while in the evenings. I didn't start getting into books until I got locked up. Being on the streets the way I was didn't allow me time to sit down and enjoy a book. Reading kept me up with what was happening in the world. Yes, I knew that most of it was made up, but I didn't let that stop me from sticking my nose to a good book. Plus, I liked to take books back to my cell and read before sleeping.

Lastly, there was dinner and then lights out. Dinner in the prison cafeteria mirrored breakfast – a rushed affair with uninspiring food.

This was my experience day in and day out for the last 15 years. This was starting to get old, but I had another five years to do the same daily.

The scorching sun beat down on the sprawling prison yard as I trudged along, the weight of the lawnmower resting heavily on my shoulders. I had just finished cutting the grass, and the sweat-drenched my prison uniform. Every step I took felt like a battle against the sweltering heat, but this was my daily routine, and I had grown accustomed to it over the years.

The rhythmic hum of the lawnmower faded into the distance as I approached the maintenance shed. With relief, I sat the machine down and wiped my brow with the back of my hand. The task was done, and I couldn't deny the satisfaction of completing a job, no matter how mundane. It gave me a sense of purpose in this confined world.

After storing away the lawnmower, I returned to my

dormitory. The walk felt endless, but I knew a refreshing shower awaited me. The prison was not the most welcoming place, but I had learned to appreciate the small moments of comfort and solitude.

The rusty showerheads in the communal bathroom did little to ease the oppressive heat that permeated the prison walls, but they were a respite from the unforgiving sun outside. As I stood beneath the lukewarm water, I let it wash away the dirt and sweat, if only temporarily. My mind wandered to the evening ahead, and the anticipation of the football game we had planned to watch lifted my spirits.

The cafeteria buzzed with activity as I approached the lunch line. I grabbed a tray and joined the line of inmates shuffling toward the serving counter. The cafeteria staff dished out the usual unappetizing prison fare, and I couldn't help but suppress a grimace as I accepted my tray. It was far from gourmet, but it filled the stomach, and that's all we could hope for here.

Sitting at a crowded table, I joined a group of fellow inmates eagerly discussing the upcoming football game. The New Orleans Saints were playing the Dallas Cowboys, an exciting matchup. Football was a rare escape from the harsh reality of prison, a fleeting connection to the world beyond these walls.

As I dug into my meal, I couldn't help but get caught up in the lively conversation. We analyzed the strengths and weaknesses of each team, debated over who would emerge victorious, and placed friendly wagers that meant nothing in the grand scheme of things but added a layer of excitement to our otherwise monotonous lives.

Once lunch was over, I decided to forego the recreation period. The sun outside had intensified, turning the prison yard into an unforgiving furnace. I was never a fan of the relentless heat, and today's scorching temperatures only reinforced my decision to remain indoors. Instead, I went to the prison library, hoping to pass the time with a good book.

When I entered the library, something caught my eye. It wasn't a book or a familiar face but the librarian. A new woman had taken over the position, and I couldn't help but be taken aback by her beauty. Her dark hair framed her face perfectly, and her eyes held a depth that seemed to invite exploration. She was an enchanting presence amidst the sterile library shelves.

My heart raced as I approached the librarian's desk. I tried to gather my thoughts, knowing that I should introduce myself. After all, there was no harm in making a new acquaintance, especially in a place like this.

"Hey there," I began, sounding casual, "I'm Tesean Carter. I don't think I've seen you around here before."

The librarian looked up from her desk, her eyes meeting mine. For a moment, there was a flicker of surprise in her gaze, and I hoped that maybe I had piqued her interest. She offered a polite but reserved smile.

"I'm Sophie," she replied, her voice soft and measured. "I just started working here a few days ago."

"New in town, huh?" I continued, trying to keep the conversation flowing. "You getting used to this place?"

Sophie nodded, her smile remaining friendly but guarded. "It's quite different from my previous job, but I'm adjusting."

Encouraged by her response, I pressed on. "Well, if you need help with anything or have questions about the inmates, feel free to ask. I've been here for a while and know the ropes."

Sophie's gaze softened, and she seemed to relax slightly. "Thank you, Tesean. I appreciate that."

With newfound confidence, I decided to take a chance and flirt. "You know, I've got some free time now. If you ever want to chat, you can always find me in the library."

Sophie's smile wavered momentarily, and I could sense a hint of unease in her eyes. She cleared her throat and replied, "I appreciate the offer, Tesean, but I must stay focused on my work. It's important to maintain professionalism here."

Her words hit me like a cold shower. I had been flirting, and she had been courteous but clear in her rejection. I felt embarrassed and disappointed, but I also respected her decision. After all, we were in a prison, and boundaries had to be maintained.

"Of course," I said, trying to mask my disappointment with a smile. "I understand. If you ever change your mind, I'll be right here."

Sophie nodded and returned to her work, and I walked away from the desk, my pride slightly bruised but my respect for her professionalism intact.

As I perused the library shelves, I couldn't help but feel a mixture of emotions. I had been captivated by Sophie's beauty and had mustered the courage to approach her, but I had also learned the importance of respecting boundaries in a place like this. With its rows of books and newfound librarian, the library had taken on a different significance. It was no longer just a place to escape through literature; it was now a reminder of the unattainable beauty beyond the prison walls.

The hours passed slowly as I immersed myself in a book, trying to lose myself in words and escape the confinement of my surroundings. I had almost forgotten about the upcoming football game and the camaraderie that awaited me back in my dorm.

When I left the library, the sun had descended toward the horizon. The prison yard had transformed from a blistering inferno to a slightly more tolerable environment, but I had no regrets about missing recreation time. Instead, I headed straight to the dorm day room, where the atmosphere was excited.

As I approached the table where my fellow inmates had gathered, they enthusiastically greeted me. The anticipation for the game was palpable, and everyone was eager to see their favorite teams compete. I took my seat, and the friendly banter and predictions continued.

The New Orleans Saints and the Dallas Cowboys were both well-loved in this group, and the rivalry between their fans added to the excitement. The room was filled with voices, each person passionately defending their team's chances and trading good-natured insults.

As the game kicked off on the small television in the corner of the room, I sat back and enjoyed the festivities of the evening.

Chapter 3

The days in this prison had churned on, each blending into the next with a repetitive rhythm that grated against the walls of my mind. The mornings dawned in the same dreary fashion, yet today held a different allure. It wasn't just the pages left unturned from the books I had borrowed the day before, but the anticipation of glimpsing Sophie again that lured me back to the library.

The corridors whispered their usual echoes as I stepped towards the library, the scent of weathered paper and the faint musk of old bindings pulling me in like a magnet. I hadn't finished the books from my previous visit, but the chance to encounter Sophie was a magnetic pull stronger than any unturned page.

As I pushed open the door, the scene unfolded like a recurring dream. Sophie, adorned with a determination that softened her features, was wrestling with a cluster of boxes near the librarian's desk. Her caramel-colored skin glowed under the flickering fluorescent lights, casting a radiant hue across the otherwise somber room.

Without hesitation, I moved closer, eager to assist her once more. "Need a hand with those?" My voice, roughened by years of confinement, carried a soft edge as I offered help.

Sophie glanced up, a fleeting expression of surprise crossing her face before she regained her composure. "I've got it," she replied briskly, her tone unwavering.

Undeterred, I reached for one of the heavier boxes, lifting it effortlessly. "I insist. Let me help."

There was a pause, a moment of contemplation in her gaze, before she reluctantly conceded, allowing me to assist her. Together, we maneuvered the boxes onto the shelves, and our interaction was limited to brief exchanges about library organization. With each exchanged word, I found myself stealing glances at her, admiring her resilience and grace.

Despite my initial caution, the temptation to flirt with Sophie lingered. A playful comment was poised on the tip of my tongue, ready to breach the formalities, yet her warning from yesterday echoed in my mind. I hesitated, deciding against it, sensing the fragility of our delicate rapport.

"Careful now, Tesean," she cautioned, her voice carrying a firmness that left no room for negotiation. "I won't hesitate to have you written up."

I raised my hands in mock surrender, a smile tugging at the corners of my lips. "Understood, Sophie. Just lending a hand."

Her lips curved in a barely perceptible nod before she redirected her attention to the shelves, leaving me to admire her from a distance.

The sheer elegance she exuded, the way she carried herself with a quiet confidence, intrigued me. I couldn't shake the lingering question of her age. Her youthful appearance contradicted the maturity she displayed. Was she in her twenties? Maybe younger, though her composed demeanor suggested otherwise. The enigma of her age continued to elude me.

As I observed her, I couldn't help but dwell on the passage of time. Fifteen long years I had slipped by within these walls, a span that had deprived me of the presence of a woman as captivating as Sophie. The memories of warmth and companionship seemed like distant echoes buried beneath the weight of incarceration.

The books lay forgotten as my mind wandered through the corridors of time, retracing moments that now seemed distant and hazy. The embrace of a loved one and the laughter shared with friends were foreign fragments of past life that felt simultaneously vivid and unreachable.

I returned to the books with a reluctant sigh, seeking solace in their familiar embrace. Each page turned was a temporary escape from the confines of reality, a fleeting moment of freedom within the prison's constraints.

Time drifted by, marked by the silent rustling of pages and

the occasional shuffle of Sophie's movements. The sun had shifted in the sky, casting elongated shadows across the library, signaling the passing hours.

As I gathered the completed books to return, I stole one final glance at Sophie. The longing persisted a yearning for a life beyond these walls, a desire for something more than fleeting encounters within the confines of a library.

With a heavy heart and unanswered questions lingering in my mind, I reluctantly departed from the library, leaving behind the enigmatic Sophie, hoping for another opportunity to cross paths, to decipher the mysteries that enveloped her, and to quell the silent ache for companionship that resonated within me.

Chapter 4

The library's whispers still echoed in my mind, mingling with the faint scent of aged paper that lingered on my fingertips. Sophie's presence, an enigmatic force, continued to weave through my thoughts, a delicate dance between attraction and caution. The allure of her resolute demeanor, the way she rebuffed my attempts at flirtation, held a curious charm that tugged at me.

I navigated the familiar corridors back to my cell, the weight of solitude hanging heavy upon my shoulders. The encounter with Sophie had sparked a longing for connection, a yearning for something more than the suffocating confines of these prison walls. Her subtle rejections only fueled the fire within, a paradoxical attraction that deepened with each denied advance.

As I neared my cell, a preoccupation with thoughts of Sophie clouded my senses, veiling my surroundings. I didn't notice the guard leading another inmate, Tyson, toward my cell until we stood face to face. The guard's introduction was brief, almost dismissive, as he left us alone within the confines of the cell.

Tyson's demeanor struck me immediately, starkly contrasting the solemnity that enveloped the rest of us within these walls. His excitement for being incarcerated, an enthusiasm that bordered on unsettling, grated against the silent rhythms of the prison. His exuberance was a stark reminder of the differences in our perceptions of this life, his enthusiasm clashing harshly with my resignation.

"Hey, man! You're Tesean, right?" Tyson's voice was loud, breaking the fragile silence I had grown accustomed to. His eyes gleamed with an odd excitement, an enthusiasm that seemed out of place within these walls.

I nodded, my gaze calm and collected. "That's me. Look, keep it down. I prefer things quiet."

Tyson's enthusiasm faltered for a moment, replaced by a puzzled expression. "Oh, sure, man! But this place, it's kinda cool, right? Like a different world!"

I sighed inwardly, a flicker of annoyance creeping in. "It's prison, Tyson. Not some adventure. Keep your excitement in check."

My words seemed to sober him slightly, and I continued, setting the boundaries that had become the unwritten rules of my solitude. "Here's how it is. I don't like extra company in this cell. I prefer quiet at night and don't share my items. Got it?"

Tyson's initial excitement dimmed as the weight of my words settled upon him. He nodded, his demeanor shifting to a more subdued tone. "Got it, man. I'll keep it down and stay out of your way."

With a nod of acknowledgment, I settled onto my bunk, the silence of the cell enveloping me once more. The echoes of Sophie's presence lingered, intertwined with the stark reality of life within these walls. The paradox of longing for connection yet cherishing solitude was a constant battle that echoed within me.

As Tyson settled into a quiet lull, the hours stretched into the silent expanse of the evening. The prison's usual hum became a distant murmur, drowned out by the thoughts that swirled within my mind. The prospect of a new cellmate and the imposition of shared space disrupted the fragile balance to which I had grown accustomed.

Sophie's image flitted through my thoughts, a beacon of intrigue amidst the desolation of my daily routine. Her refusal to entertain my advances and the caution in her demeanor only fueled the intrigue that surrounded her. A part of me relished the challenge she presented, the unattainable allure that drew me in.

However, the caution ingrained within me by years of incarceration tugged at my conscience. Getting into trouble meant risking solitary confinement, a fate I had no desire to face. The rules of this world were ruthless, and any misstep could lead to a punishment far more severe than the fleeting moments of connection I craved.

As the cell settled into a semblance of calm, I let out a resigned sigh, resigning myself to the silent echoes of solitude. Sophie's presence lingered, a distant beacon amidst the desolation of these walls, while Tyson's restless energy remained an unwelcome intrusion. The dichotomy of these contrasting presences mirrored my conflicts—a yearning for connection yet a cautious reluctance to risk the fragile balance of my existence within these confines.

Chapter 5

Tesean awoke as the first rays of dawn filtered through the narrow window of his cell. The routine of prison life had etched its pattern into his bones. With a stretch and a yawn, he sat up, rubbing the sleep from his eyes. Today was different, though. Today, he had a responsibility beyond himself.

Turning towards the new cellmate, Tyson, who was still sound asleep on the lower bunk, Tesean decided it was time for him to impart some wisdom about how things operated in their confined world. He dressed quietly, slipped on his worn-out sneakers, and approached Tyson's bunk.

"Hey, rise and shine, man," Tesean said gently, nudging Tyson's shoulder.

Tyson stirred, blinking in the dim light. "What's up?"

"Just thought I'd let you know a few things 'round here. It's important," Tesean replied, his voice low.

Over breakfast in the crowded mess hall, Tesean introduced Tyson to some of the men he knew. He had a knack for getting along with just about anyone, which showed in the other inmates' nods and smiles of recognition. Tesean's respect in the prison wasn't just earned; it was solidified through his interactions, willingness to help, and code of honor.

As they finished eating, Tesean guided Tyson through the halls, sharing tips on navigating the prison dynamics. "Respect goes a long way here, Tyson. Don't make enemies you don't need. Stick to yourself, but don't isolate too much. And whatever you do, don't start any trouble."

After the introductions, Tesean went about his day, performing his usual activities. Work in the laundry room was monotonous but provided a sense of routine. However, when the evening came, and it was time for his typical library visit, Tesean hesitated. He didn't want Sophie, the librarian, to think he was only showing up to flirt. So, he decided to opt for some fresh air instead.

Stepping outside into the prison yard, he relished the open space, the air heavy with the scent of sweat and concrete. He didn't waste any time, launching into his intense workout routine. Water bags became makeshift weights, push-ups echoed against the yard's walls, and the rhythmic cadence of sit-ups filled the air. Tesean pushed himself, finding solace and focus in the physical strain.

Midway through his routine, a commotion caught his eye. Across the yard, Tyson was embroiled in an altercation with a group of men. Tesean's brows furrowed in concern as he quickly wrapped up his exercises and hurried over.

"Hey, hey, what's going on here?" Tesean's authoritative voice cut through the tension.

Tyson looked both defensive and startled; his fists clenched at his sides. "They were disrespecting me, man!"

Tesean stepped between Tyson and the group, addressing both parties calmly. "This isn't how things work. Starting fights isn't going to earn you respect, Tyson. It's going to bring more trouble for you and others. You gotta keep a level head in here."

The other men grumbled but dispersed, leaving Tyson and Tesean standing in the aftermath of the confrontation. Tesean's expression softened, his voice taking on a more advisory tone. "You're new here, I get it. But you have to learn to pick your battles. Sometimes, it's better to walk away. Trust me, it'll save you a lot of grief."

Tyson seemed to relax a bit, albeit still tense from the adrenaline. "Thanks, man. I just... I ain't used to this place yet."

"I know, it's tough. But you have to adapt. I can show you the ropes, but you gotta be willing to listen and learn," Tesean said, offering a hand to Tyson.

Tyson hesitated before accepting the gesture, silently acknowledging the guidance being extended.

As they walked back towards their block, Tesean continued to impart advice, sharing stories of his own experiences and emphasizing the importance of keeping a low profile and respecting the unspoken rules within the prison walls.

"I got your back, Tyson. Just remember what I said," Tesean reassured, patting Tyson's shoulder as they reached their cell.

As Tyson settled back onto his bunk, Tesean took a moment to reflect. He knew it was crucial to guide newcomers like Tyson to prevent unnecessary conflicts and maintain a sense of order within the prison. It was a responsibility he took seriously, knowing that sometimes a few words of wisdom could make all the difference in a place where survival depended on more than just physical strength.

Chapter 6

Weeks had slipped by since Tesean last stepped into the library. His thirst for new reads had grown insatiable, and he had devoured every book he'd previously checked out. Today, after his routine at the laundry, he took a quick shower and decided it was high time for a library visit. But, this time, he had a plan—invite Tyson along. Maybe getting him into books could redirect some of that hot-headed energy

"Hey, Tyson, you wanna check out the library with me?" Tesean asked as they lingered in their cell after work.

Still adjusting to the prison's rhythm, Tyson glanced up from his reading book. "Eh, I got nothin' better to do.

Tesean nodded, satisfied. Maybe a little time among the shelves would help temper Tyson's volatile nature

They went to the library, and Tesean returned the stack of books he'd already read. It felt good to replace them, to know he was keeping up his end of the unspoken library agreement

Sophie, the librarian, caught his eye as he perused the New Books section. She approached with a subtle curiosity dancing in her eyes.

"Hey there, Tesean. Haven't seen you around lately," Sophie said, a hint of warmth in her voice.

"Yeah, been caught up with reading; you know how it goes," Tesean replied, trying to keep his tone casual. He didn't want to delve into his reasons for staying away.

Sophie's gaze lingered as if she wanted to say more, but Tesean redirected the conversation. "Got some good new books in here. Thanks for setting up this New Books section; it makes it easier."

Sophie smiled, appreciative of the acknowledgment. "Glad you like it. Let me know if you need any recommendations."

With a nod, Tesean excused himself, sensing Sophie's unspoken thoughts. He wasn't ready to engage in more conversation, not wanting to delve into personal matters amid the library rush.

Focusing on the shelves, Tesean was immersed in a surprising collection. Alongside the established legends of street literature were fresh names and new voices adding depth to the genre. He picked up a few books, intrigued by the diversity of the titles. The allure of a new perspective was irresistible.

Glancing over, he saw Tyson skimming through books, albeit with less enthusiasm than Tesean. He hoped the experience might ease Tyson's temper, maybe give him a different outlet for his energy.

Tesean's mind wandered back to Sophie's subtle inquiry as he perused the books. He couldn't help but wonder if she genuinely missed his presence or if something was more behind her curiosity. He appreciated her concern but wasn't eager to share more about his life.

Lost in thought, he barely noticed Tyson sidling up beside him, a book in hand. "Yo, Tesean, check this out. Looks wild."

Tesean glanced at the book Tyson held—a gritty novel with a provocative title. He chuckled. "That's a bold choice, man. Hope it's a good read."

Tyson shrugged, a glimmer of interest lighting up his eyes. "Guess we'll see."

Their interaction was interrupted by Sophie's return, a slight concern still etched on her features. "Find anything good, Tesean?"

"Yeah, got a couple in mind," Tesean replied, offering a polite smile before returning to the shelves.

As they gathered their selections, Tesean noticed Sophie watching them momentarily before returning to her duties. He couldn't shake the feeling that there was more she wanted to say, but he wasn't in the mood for a heart-to-heart in the middle of the library.

With a nod to Tyson, they made their way to the checkout

counter, exchanging the books for new ones. The weight of fresh stories in his hands was comforting, a promise of new adventures waiting to be explored.

As they left the library, Tesean glanced back at Sophie, her gaze lingering on him for a moment longer than necessary. He couldn't deny a tinge of curiosity about what she wanted to express, but, for now, the escape into the world of literature beckoned louder than any unresolved conversation.

Chapter 7

$\mathcal{D}$ays melded into each other within the prison walls, each echoing a similar routine. Tesean found solace in the predictability of his activities—work, workouts, and the sanctuary of books. Tyson seemed to grasp the unspoken rules, yet his disdain for reading remained palpable. Tesean understood. He had been the same when he first entered prison, resistant to the notion of losing himself in books.

"Man, I don't get how you can spend so much time with those damn books," Tyson grumbled one evening, lounging on his bunk.

Tesean, sitting at the small table in their cell, flipped through a novel, his eyes flicking across the pages. "It's a way to escape, you know? Help pass the time."

"Yeah, well, it ain't for me," Tyson scoffed.

Tesean didn't push further. He knew that sometimes it took time for a person to find their way in such an environment

The conversation turned unexpectedly when Tyson, shifting uncomfortably, broached a different topic. "Hey, man, what's the deal with that librarian? Sophie, right? She's pretty."

Tesean paused a ripple of discomfort running through him. "Sophie's off-limits, Tyson."

Tyson raised an eyebrow. "What, she took or something?"

Tesean sighed, feeling the weight of his own conflicted emotions. "It's not about that. Relationships between inmates and staff ain't allowed. It's against the rules."

Tyson snorted. "Rules. Man, who cares about that?"

Tesean's tone grew firm. "I do. And you should, too. It ain't just about the rules; it's about respecting boundaries."

Deep down, Tesean harbored a secret desire to get to know Sophie beyond the confines of the library. He was drawn to her, her kindness and understanding resonating with something inside him. He wanted her to see beyond the prisoner facade, to understand him, but the rules loomed over any possibility.

Tyson's dismissal of the rules irked Tesean, but the truth was that his own emotions were tangled. He didn't want Tyson or anyone else encroaching on what he secretly wished for—a chance to form a genuine connection with Sophie

Silence settled between them, the weight of unspoken

thoughts lingering. Tesean buried himself in his book, trying to divert his mind from the complexity of his feelings.

As the night wore on, Tyson's words echoed in his mind. He couldn't shake the feeling that Sophie deserved better than the fleeting attention Tyson was considering. She was more than just an object of desire; she was someone Tesean yearned to understand, to connect with on a deeper level.

As Tesean went about his usual routine the following day, thoughts of Sophie lingered. He couldn't deny her pull on him, her curiosity about her life beyond the library shelves.

During his workout, as he lifted the water bags and pushed himself through his exercises, his mind kept returning to Sophie's smile and gentle mannerisms. The desire to know her more intimately fought against the realization that his position as an inmate set boundaries he couldn't cross.

Tesean's conflict brewed beneath the surface, a silent struggle between his longing for a connection and the stark reality of the prison's regulations. He couldn't help but wonder if there was a way, a chance for Sophie to see past the stigma attached to his inmate status and understand the person he was beneath it all.

Chapter 8

The crisp morning air swept through the prison's employee parking area as Tesean meticulously tended to the weeds, his hands deftly pulling at the stubborn growth. A makeshift meal sat nearby, a simple yet satisfying combination of a sandwich and an apple. His attention, however, was diverted by the sudden appearance of an all-black Mercedes AMG GLE 53 gliding into the lot.

Tesean paused, momentarily intrigued. Vehicles of such luxury were rare in these parts, especially among those employed at the prison. He mulled over who might own such a car, mind meandering through a list of possibilities. The person behind the wheel would undoubtedly possess wealth, a stark contrast to the usual grievances aired by prison staff about their earnings.

As the car came to a halt and the door opened, Tesean's astonishment peaked when Sophie emerged. Clad in an outfit tailored for the cool Mississippi fall, she embodied effortless comfort and style. She wore a camel-colored oversized knit sweater, its softness evident even from a distance. Beneath it, dark denim jeans hugged her figure while ankle boots completed the look, their heels clicking lightly against the pavement. A scarf, loosely draped around her neck, added a touch of sophistication. Despite the casual ensemble, there was an air of refined elegance about her.

Sophie approached, her presence commanding attention. Tesean, momentarily taken aback by the sight, managed a nod of acknowledgment before she addressed him. "Hey there, Tesean," she greeted with a warm smile.

"Morning, Sophie," Tesean replied, his voice reflecting both surprise and admiration. "Nice ride you got there."

"Thank you," she replied, her tone hinting amusement. "Listen, could you swing by the library today when free? I'd like to have a chat."

Tesean, not one to shirk his duties, promised to visit after work, determined to maintain his routine despite the intrigue of the encounter. As Sophie strolled away, heading toward the prison building, Tesean noticed an inquisitive fellow inmate sauntering over.

"What was that all about, man?" the inmate queried, a note of curiosity in his voice.

Tesean, feeling a tad irked by the intrusion, brushed off the question. "None of your business. Get back to your work," he retorted, his tone leaving no room for further discussion.

The day progressed with its usual monotony, tasks, and responsibilities, keeping Tesean occupied. Yet, there was an undercurrent of anticipation as the hours trickled by, the promise to meet Sophie lingering in his mind.

The day at the prison had finally ended, and Tesean, with a sense of accomplishment, wrapped up his work. The familiar routine of gathering his belongings signaled the transition from the day's toil to a moment of respite. He knew the value of shedding the layers of labor before stepping into the realm of books and quiet conversations.

The desire to wash away the grime and sweat drove him to the communal showers, an oasis within the confines of the dorm. His solitary cleansing ritual wasn't merely about physical hygiene; it was a symbolic act of shedding the day's toil, purging the musk of labor that clung to him like a second skin.

Dressed in fresh attire, he ventured toward the library, a sanctuary that promised escape and exploration. This time, the journey to the library was solitary, devoid of Tyson's company, as his friend opted for a moment of solace amidst the outdoor expanse

Entering the library, Tesean began his usual routine, navigating through the shelves for literary companionship. He returned the books he had previously borrowed, their pages having imparted knowledge and escapades that momentarily freed him from the confines of his reality.

As he perused the array of titles, an unexpected call broke through the quiet ambiance of the library. "Tesean," the voice called out from behind him, soft yet distinct.

Turning on his heel, Tesean's gaze met Sophie's, her gesture signaling him over to the table where she sat surrounded by a stack of books. His steps, guided by curiosity, led him toward her, his mind intrigued by the sight of her engrossed in the world of literature.

"Hey, Sophie," Tesean greeted, a subtle smile curving his lips as he approached her table.

"Good to see you again," she replied warmly, her eyes lifting from the book she had been perusing moments ago. "I thought you might be interested in these," she continued, gesturing to the pile of books beside her. "They cover a range of topics, from history to fiction. Thought you might find something intriguing."

Tesean, appreciating her thoughtfulness, perused the assortment of books she had selected. His eyes scanned the titles and covers, each offering a glimpse into a different realm —histories untold, stories waiting to unfold, and worlds yet to be discovered.

"Thanks, Sophie," Tesean replied gratefully, selecting some books that piqued his interest. "I'll give these a read."

Their conversation meandered, weaving through the pages of literature and venturing into realms beyond the prison's walls. Sophie's passion for books was evident in every word she spoke, her enthusiasm infectious as they discussed various authors and genres, and the sheer joy of getting lost in a story.

As the evening waned into a quiet hum within the library, Tesean was engrossed in conversation with Sophie, their exchanges transcending the mundane confines of prison life. Time slipped away unnoticed, the words flowing freely between them, forming an unexpected bond forged amidst the shelves of books.

Eventually, the library's closing hour approached, signaling the end of their rendezvous. With a sense of reluctance, Tesean bid Sophie farewell, a newfound appreciation for their encounters settling within him.

Exiting the library, Tesean felt a shift within himself. The day had begun with routine, but it ended with an unexpected connection—a connection not confined by the prison's walls, one that held the promise of shared interests and conversations beyond the confines of their current reality.

As he returned to the dormitory, the books in hand felt like more than just a collection of pages and words. They were tokens of a burgeoning connection, a bridge between two worlds that, despite their disparities, found common ground within the pages of literature.

Chapter 9

The library had become more than a haven for Tesean. It was his solace, a sanctuary where the barriers of prison life momentarily dissolved, thanks to Sophie. From the moment she'd invited him to the library, a bond had woven between them, growing stronger with each visit.

Tesean's three-times-a-week commitment to the library had become a ritual, a rhythmic dance he eagerly performed to spend time with Sophie. He'd adjusted his schedule, not wanting to raise suspicion that their friendship could violate any rules. Yet, with each exchange of smiles and shared moments between the bookshelves, Tesean's heart grew fonder.

With her infectious passion for books and caring nature,

Sophie became a beacon of light in Tesean's confined world. He found himself yearning for her company, cherishing their conversations, and secretly nurturing a hope for something more.

As the days passed, their bond deepened, but uncertainty lingered in Tesean's heart. He dreamed of a future with Sophie beyond the prison walls, but he was unsure if she saw the same potential in their relationship.

With Christmas approaching, Tesean found himself again in the library amidst the scent of aged paper and the comforting silence. Sophie's voice pulled him from his reverie, beckoning him over with an invitation to explore a new book. The title, "Down to Ride, Ride: An Urban Mississippi Romance," intrigued Tesean. The prospect excited him because he'd never read literature from his home state.

As Sophie handed him the book, she mentioned her absence until the new year, urging him to start reading that night. Tesean's heart sank at the thought of not seeing her for weeks, his anticipation for the book dampened by the longing to be near her.

Lost in his emotions, he left the library, only to discover later in his cell that Sophie had given him two copies of the same book. Confusion intertwined with a strange sense of disappointment. He realized the actual gift wasn't the book itself but the connection it represented, the shared moments between the pages that would now have to sustain him until her return.

A whirlwind of emotions surged as Tesean stared at the duplicate books. The ache of missing Sophie mingled with the excitement of diving into a new story. He couldn't deny the hollow feeling that came with her absence. Then, he understood the depth of his feelings for her, which stretched far beyond friendship.

In the quiet solitude of his cell, Tesean opened one of the copies of "Down to Ride, Ride." As he delved into the pages, he found himself immersed in a tale that mirrored the complexities of his emotions. The characters' journey paralleled his internal struggles, their love story resonating deeply within his heart.

As Tesean devoured the book's chapters in the following weeks, Sophie's absence loomed over him. He found himself contemplating their connection, realizing how much her presence had come to mean to him. His mind wandered to a future where they could walk freely, no longer bound by prison walls.

The turning of each page marked the passage of time, each word a testament to the evolving feelings within him. Tesean couldn't help but wonder if Sophie felt the same pull of their connection transcended the boundaries of their current circumstances.

Tesean's fingers trembled as he gingerly opened the second copy of "Down to Ride, Ride," his curiosity piqued by the oddity of two identical books. To his bewilderment, as he flipped through the pages, he discovered a carefully hollowed-out space, revealing a sleek cell phone nestled within. Shock surged through him; the realization of possessing contraband inside the prison walls struck him hard. Yet, amidst the swirling mix of fear and astonishment, a rush of warmth flooded his heart. Sophie had orchestrated this clandestine gift, a lifeline that defied the rules, solely to maintain their connection during her absence. Gratitude and joy washed over him, knowing she'd risked so much to ensure they could still talk while she was away. It was a daring act of affection that simultaneously thrilled and unsettled him, but he now understood why Sophie kept insisting that he started reading the book that night.

Chapter 10

In the dead of night, with the dorm enveloped in silence and darkness, Tesean waited. He waited until the air grew still until every sound faded into a peaceful lullaby of slumber. Only then did he dare to power on the phone. His heart hammered in his chest as he cautiously navigated through the device, knowing the risks he was taking by simply holding it in his hands.

First, he set a passcode, fingers moving swiftly across the screen to ensure this forbidden treasure remained a secret. The phone's glowing screen seemed to taunt him, an illicit beacon amid the prison's enforced rules. With a sense of urgency, he muted it entirely, not even allowing a vibration to betray its presence. Trust was a rare commodity in this confined world, and Tesean knew better than to leave anything to chance, especially when Tyson, his cellmate, could easily stumble upon this contraband.

A notification blinked insistently, drawing Tesean's attention. An unopened message from an unknown number hung tantalizingly in the air. His heart raced as he cautiously tapped the screen, revealing a text from Sophie. Her words danced across the screen, a clandestine message woven with warmth and care. She implored him to text her as soon as he found her message. Tesean wasted no time responding, relief flooding him as he confirmed receipt of the phone and expressed gratitude for her daring gesture.

Within moments, Sophie's reply adorned the screen with smiling emojis, their brightness contrasting against the dimly lit cell. A simple acknowledgment unfolded into a string of messages spanned the night. In the quiet solitude of his cell, Tesean and Sophie embarked on a journey of words, their conversation an oasis in the desert of isolation.

They exchanged thoughts, dreams, and snippets of their day, weaving an invisible thread that bridged the physical distance between them. Tesean found solace in Sophie's messages, each word a lifeline connecting him to a world beyond the prison walls. He couldn't help but wonder at her audacity, at the lengths she'd gone to ensure their communication persisted.

As the night wore on, Tesean's guard slowly softened, his reservations melting away with each exchange. He dared to ask her why she risked so much to bring the phone into the prison. Sophie's reply resonated with sincerity; she wanted to maintain their connection while she was away. Her words carried a weight of devotion that stirred something profound within Tesean.

THEIR CONVERSATION WOVE a tapestry of shared laughter, contemplative musings, and stolen moments of intimacy. Time seemed to lose its meaning as they delved deeper into their exchange, their messages a sanctuary amidst the confines of their separate worlds.

With every text, Tesean found himself drawn closer to Sophie, the invisible barriers that separated them dissolving with each word typed and received. The forbidden phone became a vessel for their burgeoning connection, a symbol of their shared desire to defy the constraints imposed by their circumstances.

That night, Sophie sent Tesean a video of her touching herself. She appeared to be getting ready to take a shower. After propping the phone up, she closed the lid on the toilet and sat down. Sophie put one foot on the tub's edge and held the other up so high that it rested on the front of her shoulder. She squeezed her breast with one hand and spread her pussy lips apart with the other, pinching her nipple and playing with her clit. That shit was so fucken sexy to Tesean that his dick stood at attention. He was hot and bothered, so sleep was no longer an option.

Tesean gripped the base of his dick and began to stroke its length. He imagined that both he and Sophie were unable to take their eyes off the exquisite sexual drama that was being played out as if they were in person. Tesean went into a zone and started jacking his dick off with speed and force while Sophie slipped a second finger into her dripping wet pussy. His dick pulsed once and made his toes ball up. "Fuck," he suddenly mouthed as a load of cum shot all over the makeshift curtain.

Sophie became tense and started convulsing madly as an orgasm shuddered through her body. "AHHHHSSSSHHHIII-ITTTT!!!" she sang as her eyes rolled into the back of her head.

THE FOLLOWING DAY, Tesean woke up with a jolt, his mind immediately racing back to his conversation with Sophie the night before. Despite their communication limitations, their connection felt tangible, as if each text message brought them closer together.

He lay in bed replaying the details of their conversation in his mind. Sophie had shared her aspirations, dreams, and desires for the future, and he found himself relating to her on a level he hadn't expected. It was a rare opportunity for him to connect with someone beyond the confines of his prison life.

With cautious excitement, Tesean proceeded through his

day as inconspicuously as possible, keeping his cell phone hidden in a spot that no one would suspect. His routine remained unchanged, blending into the rhythms of prison life while his thoughts frequently drifted back to the anticipation of a response from Sophie.

As evening descended and the prison settled into its nightly routine, Tesean covertly retrieved his cell phone, waiting until the silence of the night enveloped the corridors. He messaged Sophie, eager to hear about her day and hoping she'd share even the most minor details.

In the quiet of his cell, with only the dim light from his phone illuminating his face, Tesean's heart raced as he awaited Sophie's reply. In these stolen moments of connection, he found solace and a flicker of hope amidst the confines of his current reality.

In the subdued ambiance of his cell, Tesean's phone illuminated, displaying Sophie's message. Her recounting the day and the snapshots from her shopping expedition brought joy to his otherwise confined existence. As he absorbed the images, each one felt like a glimpse into a world far removed from the prison walls. Yet, alongside the fleeting happiness was a sense of cautious restraint. Aware of the risk posed by these digital souvenirs, Tesean promptly removed the images from his phone. He didn't dare risk their discovery. Instead, he committed the details to memory, cherishing each moment captured in those pictures, safeguarded in the recesses of his mind where no one else could tread.

On Christmas Eve, palpable anticipation lingered within the prison walls as some inmates eagerly awaited holiday packages from their families. For Tesean, this day, he had never received anything before. Yet, amidst the chorus of names being called, he was taken aback when his own echoed through the corridor. Perplexed, he made his way to claim the unexpected parcel, emblazoned with the name 'Shann Gee.' Confusion initially clouded his thoughts, puzzled by the unfamiliar sender. Then, like a sudden revelation, realization struck —a clever alias that stirred recognition. It was Sophie, using the pseudonym of the author whose book she had gifted him, an ingenious gesture that brought a surge of emotions and unexpected warmth to his heart.

Within the carefully wrapped holiday package, he laid a thoughtful assortment of items, each bearing a significance that resonated deeply with Tesean. Nestled among the contents were an array of snacks—small indulgences in a place where such luxuries were scarce. Personal hygiene items, meticulously chosen, spoke volumes of care and consideration. Alongside these essentials were prison-issued clothing items, a practical addition that didn't go unnoticed. Tesean felt a surge of gratitude and emotion, knowing that Sophie had gone to such lengths to ensure he felt remembered and cared for during this holiday season. The gesture filled him with a profound sense of joy and appreciation. Anticipation brewed within him, eager for the inevitable lockdown when he could express his heartfelt gratitude to Sophie for her kindness.

In the quiet solitude of his cell, Tesean carefully typed out a heartfelt thank-you message to Sophie, expressing his overwhelming gratitude for the unexpected care package. He conveyed how her thoughtful gesture had touched him deeply, noting that it was the first time in his fifteen years behind bars that someone had thought of him during the holiday season. He poured his emotions into the text, conveying his appreciation for her kindness in a place where such gestures were rare. With genuine sincerity, he promised to repay her kindness someday, a vow that echoed his desire to reciprocate the warmth and generosity she had shown him during a time when it mattered the most.

As the morning light filtered into the cell, Tesean stirred awake to an unsettling sight—his cellmate, Tyson, rifling through the contents of the holiday package Sophie had sent. Instant anger surged within Tesean, his voice firm as he reminded Tyson about the unspoken rule of prison etiquette: never intrude into another man's belongings. Caught off guard, Tyson quickly apologized, seemingly remorseful for his intrusion. However, as the moment passed, a heavy realization settled upon Tesean. Trust, once fractured, was not quickly rebuilt within the confines of these walls. He understood the weight of this breach—a violation of personal boundaries tantamount to theft. From that moment forward, he knew he'd have to keep a vigilant eye on Tyson, recognizing that his sense of security had been compromised.

Tesean couldn't shake off the lingering frustration and unease after catching Tyson in his personal belongings. The breach of trust weighed heavily on his mind, creating a cloud of discontent that followed him throughout the day. Despite his reservations, he couldn't help but notice the evident remorse in Tyson's demeanor. Sensing an opportunity for clarity, Tesean gestured to Tyson, silently asking him to step aside for a conversation.

Tesean's voice was measured but firm as he addressed Tyson, his expression a mix of disappointment and caution. "Look, Tyson, what happened earlier... it's not something I can just let slide."

Tyson shifted uncomfortably, his eyes conveying a mixture of regret and remorse. "Man, I'm real sorry, Tesean. I didn't mean to cross a line. I was just curious, you know?"

Tesean nodded, acknowledging the apology. "I get it, but, in here, boundaries mean everything. It's about trust, which I can't just hand out freely anymore. It's going to take time."

Tyson's tone softened, his regret palpable. "I understand, Tesean. I messed up and will do whatever it takes to make it right."

Tesean sighed, the weight of the situation evident in his gaze. "I hear you, but actions speak louder than words. Trust isn't something that comes easily in this place. You'll have to earn it back, Tyson. It's not going to happen overnight."

Tyson nodded solemnly, understanding the gravity of the situation. "I'll do my best, man. I really will."

With a nod of acknowledgment, Tesean turned away, the air heavy with the understanding that trust, once broken, was a fragile thing to rebuild within the confines of their shared cell. Tyson's continued apologies echoed in the space, but Tesean knew that time and consistent actions would determine whether their trust could be restored.

Chapter 12

In the days that followed, Tyson made a concerted effort to rebuild the trust that had frayed between him and Tesean. Understanding Tesean's frustration with his actions, Tyson was determined to mend their bond. He took deliberate steps to demonstrate his reliability, showing up when needed and following through on his promises to Tesean. Despite Tesean's initial irritation, Tyson remained steadfast, patient, and committed to regaining his friend's confidence. Tesean, recognizing Tyson's genuine efforts, eventually acknowledged the sincerity behind Tyson's actions. In a moment of understanding, Tesean reassured Tyson that fate had its way of unfolding, believing their relationship would find its rightful path.

As the holiday season drew close, Tesean felt contentment

knowing that Sophie was back at work. Her presence added a familiar and comforting rhythm to the prison that had been missing during the festive break. Energized by new opportunities, Tesean stumbled upon a job opening at the prison library, which held a special allure for him. Encouraged by his aspirations and motivated to be close to Sophie, Tesean promptly contacted his case worker to navigate the application process. The chance to contribute to a space filled with knowledge and stories resonated deeply with Tesean, igniting a renewed sense of purpose and excitement for the future.

With determination and anticipation, Tesean approached Sophie, sharing his intention to apply for the position at the prison library. Sophie, always supportive and understanding, listened attentively as Tesean expressed his enthusiasm for the role. Promising to do what she could to assist him, Sophie assured Tesean that she'd keep an eye out for his case worker, understanding the significance of her influence in the hiring process for the library. As someone overseeing the operations there, Sophie held the decisive power in selecting the library's staff, and she wanted nothing more than to spend time with Tesean.

Tesean: Hey, Ms. Johnson, I wanted to talk to you about something. I'm interested in applying for that job opening at the prison library.

Ms. Johnson: (Surprised) The library? That's unexpected, Tesean. You've been doing great with the outdoor work.

Tesean: Yeah, I know, but I've been thinking. I love books,

you know? And being out in the sun all day, it's getting tough. I could do more with something I enjoy.

Ms. Johnson: (Understanding) I see. It's essential to find work that aligns with your passions. Let me talk to the prison library director. I'll advocate for you, Tesean, and see what I can do.

Tesean: Thanks, Ms. Johnson. I appreciate it. This means a lot to me.

Ms. Johnson: I'll reply as soon as I've spoken with them. Keep your hopes up, Tesean. You never know what opportunities might come your way.

Lying on his bunk, he got comfortable, and his mind drifted to Sophie. He wondered what it would be like working with her in the library. As he drifted to sleep, he couldn't help but imagine walking up on her as she placed books on the shelf. When he approached her, he spun her around and bent her over the ladder she used to reach the top shelves.

"You know I want you, right?" he growled, slapping his semi-hard dick across her thick ass cheeks repeatedly. "Let me show you I want you!" he spat, lifting one of her thighs on the crest of his arm. Tesean pushed his dick inside Sophie's warm pussy and fucked her roughly from behind.

"Tesean!" she whined. "Baby, slow down!"

"Shhhhh, before you get us caught!" He slapped her ass cheek and watched it jiggle. He fucked her so hard and quick that they almost lost balance. Tesean felt his nut tingling. The pounding sound his forceful thrusts were making against

Sophie's ass cheeks was intoxicating. He pounded repeatedly until she silently begged for God! He stopped and gave her three final pumps! ONE!

"Tesean," she whimpered his name.

TWO!

"FUUUUUCK!" she continued.

THREE!!! He pumped.

"EWWWWW!!!" She tapped repeatedly on the bookshelf that she was using to hold her, as Tesean pulled out and nutted on her booty.

Chapter 13

Tesean entered the prison library, a realm of knowledge bound by towering shelves filled with books of every imaginable genre. The air, thick with the scent of aged paper, held promises of new beginnings. It was his first day on the job, and a sense of purpose surged within him.

Sophie greeted him with a warm smile, her presence illuminating the room like a beacon of familiarity amidst the confines of the prison. "Glad you're here, Tesean," she said, reassuring and encouraging. "Let's get started."

His daily routine soon became a rhythm. Mornings would find him at the front desk, checking inmates in and out, his demeanor a blend of deference and attentiveness. "Morning, Jones. Here for your next read?" Tesean would ask, handing over a requested novel to an inmate, their familiarity growing with each interaction.

Handling book requests became his forte, meticulously cataloging and organizing the library's inventory. He'd take notes of inmates' preferences, eager to fulfill their literary cravings. "Sophie, we're running low on the classics," Tesean mentioned one afternoon, pointing to a shelf with tattered copies of timeless tales.

"I'll make a note to order more," Sophie replied, acknowledging his diligence.

Yet, amidst the stacks of books and the hum of prison life, Tesean found his favorite moments woven within the hours spent alongside Sophie. Their camaraderie blossomed into a friendship that transcended the library's confines. Sophie's guidance and support were invaluable, her expertise guiding Tesean through the nuances of the job.

Their bond extended beyond the library's walls. Evenings often found their phones lighting up with messages exchanged between them. "Just finished 'To Kill a Mockingbird.' It was incredible," Sophie texted one night.

"Isn't it? The lessons in that book are timeless," Tesean replied, their conversation meandering through literary discussions and personal anecdotes.

Despite spending the entire day together during the week, the connection between Tesean and Sophie thrived, their texts a continuation of the rapport they shared. "Found a hidden gem today. Can't wait for you to read it," Sophie messaged, igniting Tesean's curiosity.

Their friendship became an anchor in Tesean's life, a source of joy and comfort amidst the confines of the prison's routine. Whether discussing books, sharing stories from their respective lives, or exchanging lighthearted banter, their bond deepened, transcending their workplace constraints.

Working in the library had opened a new chapter in Tesean's life—one filled with the joy of being surrounded by books and the immeasurable value of a genuine connection with Sophie. In her presence, he found solace, inspiration, and a sense of belonging that surpassed the confines of their professional roles.

As days turned into weeks, Tesean's enthusiasm for his work in the prison library grew, fueled by his love for books and cherished moments spent alongside Sophie. Their bond had become an integral part of his daily life, an unwavering support system that buoyed his spirits, transforming his days within the prison walls into a sanctuary of shared laughter, learning, and friendship.

Chapter 14

Tesean's friends gathered during their break; a jovial atmosphere enveloped the conversation. The topic of Tesean's recent job switch surfaced, prompting playful teasing from his buddies. "Working in the prison library, huh?" one laughed. "Never thought you'd choose a job that'd put you to sleep!"

Tesean chuckled along, accustomed to their good-natured banter. "Yeah, yeah, laugh all you want," he quipped back, shrugging off their jests. Yet, beneath the lighthearted facade, Tesean harbored a truth he kept guarded—his fondness for his new workplace wasn't solely about the books.

The teasing continued, but as the day wound down and Tesean returned to his cell, his thoughts drifted to the real reason behind his choice. The library wasn't just a place of employment; it was where his connection with Sophie blossomed. He cherished their moments together, her guidance, and the unspoken camaraderie that had grown between them.

As he settled into his cell, Tyson, his cellmate, approached him. "Hey, man, I've been thinking," Tyson began, a tinge of earnestness in his voice. "I need to do something, stay busy, you know? Keep out of trouble."

Tesean listened, understanding the importance of finding purpose within the prison's confines. "I get it, Ty. I'll see what I can do," he replied, contemplating how to help his friend navigate the prison's limited opportunities.

During his library shift, Tesean pondered Tyson's predicament the following day. He knew the outside crew had openings and a more relaxed atmosphere, offering a chance for inmates to engage positively. It was a gateway to connect with those who had found their balance within the system.

"Sophie!" Tesean called, catching her attention during a brief respite. "I've got a friend, Tyson. He's looking for something productive to do. You think there might be an opening for him with the outside crew?"

Sophie considered his request, recognizing Tesean's genuine concern for his friend's well-being. "I'll look into it. Can't make any promises, but I'll see what options are available," she assured, appreciating Tesean's willingness to advocate for his friend.

Days passed, and Sophie approached Tesean with a nod.

"Got word from the crew supervisor. They're willing to give Tyson a shot," she relayed, a small smile on her lips.

Tesean felt relief knowing that Tyson would have a chance to occupy his time constructively. He shared the news with Tyson, who expressed gratitude and a newfound sense of purpose. Tesean knew that connecting Tyson with the outside crew might introduce him to a different crowd, one that embraced positivity amidst the challenges of incarceration.

In the quiet moments of the evening, after the library closed and the day's duties were done, Tesean reflected on the threads that wove through his life in the prison. His bond with Sophie had led him to a job that brought him fulfillment beyond the confines of his cell. And now, through his connection with Sophie, he had found a way to guide Tyson toward a path that offered hope and a chance for transformation.

As the night settled in and Tesean exchanged a brief text with Sophie, he couldn't help but acknowledge their growing friendship's profound impact on shaping his life and those around him. It wasn't just about the books or the job—the connections forged within the prison walls that held the promise of redemption and a shared journey toward a better tomorrow.

Lying down for the night, he couldn't help but think about what it would be like if they were home together. He imagined coming home to find Sophie waiting on him, wearing only a red thong, black thigh boots, and a matching Victoria's Secret bra and whip.

"What are you going to do with that whip?" Tesean asked, laughing.

"Whip your ass if you don't obey me!" she said frankly before cracking the whip close to his leg. "Now, take that shit off, so I can look at that body!" she ordered. Her face was serious and assertive. Tesean did as he was told and stripped down to his boxers.

This made Tesean's dick rock hard to see her taking charge the way that she was.

Doing as he was told, he stripped ass naked. He could see the excitement in Sophie's eyes as she eyed him from head to toe. Her eyes lingered on his dick as she took in how big it was.

Dropping to her knees, she crawled over to him. She wrapped her full plum-colored lips around his dick and gathered his ball sack in one of her palms. Sophie was determined to tackle that big, long, bad boy; just the tip was damn near in the back of her throat. She tried to fit a little more in her mouth and immediately started gagging.

Shit! Tesean thought, as Sophie took a deep breath and slid its head back into her mouth. She relaxed the back of her throat and moved her warm mouth up and down his dick. She caught a rhythm and pace; then, the shit was on. She tilted her head to the side a bit and sucked in her cheeks so the sides of her jaws gave his dick an even snugger fit. No matter how hard she tried, his whole dick would not fit into her mouth, so she licked the remainder of his shaft from time to time to keep it slick while she wrapped her hands around it to jack him off in her mouth. She had to use both hands, which was a first for her, but the head that she gave was fire and she was working with it. Tesean was in a state of shock and bliss at the same time. *Damn!* he thought to himself. He couldn't wait until the day this dream could come true.

Chapter 15

In the library's familiar embrace, Tesean immersed himself in the quiet rhythm of organizing shelves and assisting inmates with book selections. Sophie's presence was a constant source of comfort, her guidance shaping his understanding of the library's intricate workings. As days turned into weeks, a subtle shift colored their interactions—a delicate dance of playful banter and shared glances that spoke volumes in their silent language.

Tesean couldn't deny the growing affection he harbored for Sophie. Their connection had blossomed beyond the confines of mere friendship. He found himself stealing fleeting glances at her. At the same time, she busied herself with library tasks, her laughter echoing through the space, captivating him in a way that transcended the boundaries of their professional relationship.

With Valentine's Day approaching, Tesean's thoughts were consumed by the desire to express his feelings for Sophie. But the weight of limited finances loomed heavily over him. Determined to make the day memorable for her, he devised a plan—sell some of the extra food he had stored in his cell. It was a meager solution, but he was willing to sacrifice for someone who unknowingly captured his heart.

In the evenings, after the library closed, Tesean carefully sorted his belongings, selecting non-perishable items he could sell. He knew the value of what little he possessed, but the thought of making Sophie smile on Valentine's Day fueled his resolve.

As the days passed, he discreetly approached a few fellow inmates, offering snacks and canned goods at modest prices. The transactions were subtle, conversations hushed, his determination to make Sophie's day memorable outweighing any concerns about parting with his provisions.

With each sale, Tesean's anticipation for Valentine's Day grew. He imagined surprising Sophie with a small token of appreciation—a gesture conveying his admiration for her. It wasn't about the value of the gift but the sentiment behind it, a heartfelt expression of his feelings that transcended monetary worth.

At work, their interactions held an undercurrent of affection. Tesean would pass Sophie a book with a shy smile, their fingers brushing in a fleeting touch that sent sparks of electricity coursing through him. Sophie's laughter and her genuine interest in their conversations only strengthened Tesean's resolve to make the upcoming Valentine's Day memorable for her.

As the day approached, Tesean felt a mix of nervousness and excitement. On the morning of Valentine's Day, he arrived at work with a small package tucked away—a carefully wrapped parcel containing a book he knew Sophie had mentioned wanting to read. It was second-hand but in excellent condition, a testament to his thoughtful consideration. Tesean had mustered up enough money to call a long-time friend and have them order it and send it to the prison since they could receive books that came directly from the store.

During a lull in their duties, Tesean approached Sophie, his heart pounding with anticipation and apprehension. "Hey, Sophie," he began, offering her the modestly wrapped gift. "Happy Valentine's Day."

Sophie's eyes lit up with surprise and warmth as she accepted the package. "Tesean, you didn't have to," she started, but her words softened as she opened the gift. The sight of the book elicited a genuine smile from her, her gratitude evident in the sparkle of her eyes.

Tesean felt relief and joy, his heart soaring at Sophie's happiness. It wasn't the grandest of gestures, but the genuine appreciation reflected in her expression made it all worthwhile.

As the day drew close, Tesean returned to his cell, a sense of contentment settling within him. The sacrifice of parting with his food seemed insignificant compared to the joy he had brought to Sophie. In the quiet solitude of his room, he couldn't help but reflect on the moments shared with her—the subtle flirtations, the unspoken connection, and the whispered promises of something more, weaving a tapestry of affection within the confines of their world.

Chapter 16

As Tesean drifted into slumber, his mind painted vivid scenes of an alternate reality where freedom wasn't a distant dream. In his dream, Valentine's Day unfolded in a world where he could take Sophie to an intimate dinner, the ambiance adorned with flickering candlelight and soft music in the background. In the dream's embrace, he expressed his deepest emotions, pouring out his love to Sophie as he gazed into her eyes, the words flowing effortlessly from his heart. The dream felt so real, each moment etched with tenderness and authenticity.

Waking up the next day, Tesean carried remnants of the dream, a sense of longing and warmth enveloping his thoughts. Eager to share the dream's details with Sophie, he hurried to work, anticipating coursing through him. As he entered the library, his eyes sought out Sophie, eager to recount the dream that had felt so palpable as though it had transcended the boundaries of sleep to become a cherished memory.

Tesean: Hey, Sophie, I've got to tell you about this dream I had last night, purposely leaving out the sexual part.

Sophie: (Curiously) Oh? What was it about?

Tesean: It was about Valentine's Day... if I were out, you know? I took you to this super intimate dinner and told you how I felt.

Sophie: (Smiling) That sounds lovely, Tesean. A romantic dinner and heartfelt confession, huh?

Tesean: Yeah, it felt so real. I wish it could've been.

Sophie: (Comfortingly) You never know, Tesean. If things keep going as they are, who's to say that dream won't come true someday?

Tesean: (Hopeful) You think so?

Sophie: (Encouragingly) Absolutely. We'll keep moving forward, Tesean. You never know what the future holds.

Tesean: Thanks, Sophie. I just wanted to share it with you. It felt so... right.

Sophie: (Warmly) I'm glad you did. And who knows? Maybe one day, we'll make that dream a reality.

TESEAN WEARILY CONCLUDED his workday at the prison library, the hushed shuffling of books starkly contrasting the harsh reality of his surroundings. As he returned to his cell, he longed for respite. Lying down, he closed his eyes, trying to escape the oppressive atmosphere that clung to the prison walls. Suddenly, his cellmate Tyson entered, breaking the uneasy tranquility. Tyson's urgent tone conveyed a sense of imminent danger. "Tesean, we got a problem. The guards are planning a surprise search, and it's happening soon," Tyson whispered anxiously. Tesean's eyes widened in panic; he knew he had contraband hidden in the cell. As adrenaline surged, he jumped up, grappling with the impending consequences of his secret possessions as the reality of the imminent search loomed over them.

Chapter 17

The distant hum of the prison echoed through the corridors as Tesean sat on the edge of his bunk, his hands nervously tapping against his thighs. The small, inconspicuous cell phone, hidden expertly within the confines of his meager belongings, weighed heavily on his mind. A storm of anxiety brewed in his chest as he contemplated the potential consequences of being caught with this forbidden device. His eyes darted towards the dull glow from the tiny screen, currently nestled beneath a stack of worn-out books.

Tesean couldn't shake the nagging feeling that his clandestine cell phone possession was a ticking time bomb, ready to explode at the slightest provocation. As he glanced around the cramped cell, the cold, metallic bars seemed to close in on him, emphasizing the precariousness of his situation.

Sophie had sent him the contraband device in a desperate attempt to maintain a semblance of connection during his time behind bars. Tesean appreciated the gesture, longing for a lifeline to the outside world, yet the potential repercussions of being caught were daunting. The penalties for possessing a prohibited communication device in prison were severe—solitary confinement, loss of privileges, and, in some cases, extended sentences.

Tesean's thoughts swirled like a storm as he considered the grim possibilities. He imagined the stern faces of the guards, the cold, unyielding walls of a solitary cell, and the loneliness that would accompany isolation. The phone, while a lifeline, had become a source of torment, a constant reminder of the fine line he walked between connection and catastrophe.

As the night wore on, Tesean's mind grappled with conflicting desires. On the one hand, he yearned to reach out to Sophie, hear her voice, and find solace in her words' familiar cadence. On the other hand, the fear of discovery gnawed at him, warning against the potential fallout if the guards were to uncover his secret.

He knew that discretion was paramount, especially with the looming threat of a surprise cell search. Tesean paced the narrow confines of his cell, the dim overhead light casting shadows that danced in rhythm with the tumult in his mind. He contemplated the risk of bringing the phone out of its concealed hiding spot to send a brief message to Sophie, assuring her of his safety and explaining the gravity of his situation.

The metallic clang of distant cell doors being locked for the night only heightened Tesean's sense of urgency. The prison, usually a cacophony of background noise, now felt eerily silent as he grappled with the weight of his decisions. He was torn between the desire for connection and the need to preserve his fragile sense of security within the prison's unforgiving walls.

As the minutes turned into hours, Tesean decided to stay up throughout the night, hyper-vigilant and anxiously anticipating the inevitable cell search. He couldn't afford to be caught off guard, and the thought of being roused from sleep by the intrusion of guards sent shivers down his spine.

The minutes crawled by each tick of the clock, magnifying the tension in the air. Tesean sat on his bunk, his eyes fixed on the cell door, his ears tuned to the slightest sound outside. The sounds of distant footsteps and the occasional shuffle of prison personnel reverberated through the corridor, amplifying the sense of impending doom.

As the night wore on, Tesean's mind oscillated between paranoia and determination. The soft glow of the hidden-phone seemed to taunt him, a silent reminder of the risks he took to maintain a semblance of normalcy in a world defined by confinement and restriction.

In desperation, Tesean decided to draft a brief message to Sophie, carefully crafting words that conveyed the urgency of his situation and the depth of his affection for her. He cautiously typed each letter, his fingers dancing across the small screen as if navigating a minefield. Every creak of the cell door or distant echo made him freeze; the phone clutched tightly in his hand.

Despite the risks, the need to reassure Sophie overcame his fear of discovery. Tesean decided to send the message, his heart pounding as he pressed the "send" button. The seconds that followed felt like an eternity as he waited for a response, the anxiety escalating with each passing moment.

The notification sound, normally innocuous, echoed through the stillness of the cell like a gunshot. Tesean's heart skipped a beat as he cautiously checked the screen, relief washing over him when he saw Sophie's response. Her words conveyed a mix of concern and understanding, a lifeline from the world beyond the prison bars.

However, the fleeting sense of relief was quickly replaced by the realization that the sent message would remain in the phone's memory, a digital breadcrumb that could lead the guards straight to his clandestine communication. Tesean's pulse quickened, and he grappled with the consequences of his decision.

As he contemplated deleting the message, the distant echo of heavy boots and jingling keys reached his ears. Panic surged through Tesean's veins as he hastily stashed the phone back in its hiding spot, concealing it beneath the stack of books with trembling hands.

The sound of approaching footsteps grew louder, and Tesean's breath caught in his throat. The dim glow of the phone, now hidden once more, seemed to mock him as the cell door creaked open. Two uniformed guards entered, their stern expressions casting a foreboding shadow.

"Routine cell search," one of them announced the words hanging in the air like an ominous prelude. Tesean forced himself to maintain composure, his eyes fixed on the guards as they meticulously inspected every corner of the cell.

The minutes stretched into an agonizing eternity, Tesean's heart pounding with each passing second. He dared not glance toward the hidden-phone, afraid his anxiety would betray him. The guards, seemingly oblivious to the clandestine device's presence, finished their search and exited the cell without a word.

As the door closed behind them, Tesean released a breath he hadn't realized he was holding. Relief and gratitude flooded his senses with a lingering sense of trepidation. The close call served as a stark reminder of the fragility of his situation, the constant balancing act between connection and survival within the confines of the prison.

The remainder of the night unfolded in restless vigilance. Tesean sat on the edge of his bunk, his eyes fixed on the dim glow beneath the books. The fear of being caught with the cell phone loomed large, yet the desire for connection, for a life-line to the world beyond the prison walls, remained unabated.

As dawn broke, casting a muted glow through the cell's

narrow window, Tesean felt the weight of the night's events settle upon him. He had navigated the treacherous waters of concealed communication and, for now, he remained undiscovered. Yet, once a source of comfort, the phone had become a double-edged sword, its presence a constant reminder of the risks he took for a semblance of normalcy in a world defined by confinement.

Chapter 18

The following day, he arrived, bringing a lingering tension that clung to Tesean like a shadow. The narrow corridors of the prison seemed to close in on him as he made his way to his assigned workplace. Despite the routine nature of his daily tasks, the previous night's events cast a long, foreboding shadow over his thoughts.

As Tesean signed in for his work shift, the low hum of activity in the prison workplace starkly contrasted with the turmoil within him. The rhythmic sounds of machinery and the muffled conversations of fellow inmates became a backdrop to his anxious musings. The routine he had grown accustomed to felt disrupted, and a pervasive sense of vulnerability lingered.

Sophie approached him with a concerned expression as he

went about his duties. She had been informed about the surprise cell search and couldn't help but worry for his well-being. "Tesean, I heard about the search last night. Are you okay?" she asked in a hushed tone, glancing around to ensure their conversation remained discreet.

Tesean looked up from his task; the weariness etched across his features. "Yeah, Soph, I made it through without them finding the phone," he admitted, his voice carrying relief and lingering apprehension.

Sophie sighed, her worry evident in her eyes. "I'm glad they didn't find it, but you can't keep living like this, Tesean. It's too risky."

"I know, Soph, but it's the only way I can talk to you, to keep some connection to the outside," Tesean replied. His mind swiftly turned towards the hidden-phone, discreetly nestled among the books in his cell

She placed a comforting hand on his shoulder, conveying both understanding and concern. "I get it, Tesean, I do. But it's not a sustainable way to live if you're constantly on edge, worried about being caught. We need to figure out a safer way for you to have some communication."

Tesean nodded, acknowledging the truth in Sophie's words. The delicate balance he sought between connection and concealment had become increasingly precarious. The fear of being caught gnawed at him, and he constantly glanced over his shoulder, questioning the security of his clandestine communication.

As the workday progressed, the whispers of uncertainty clouded Tesean's mind. The routine tasks he once performed with ease now felt like a series of mechanical motions, his focus divided between his responsibilities and the lingering fear of discovery. The phone's weight in his pocket, a constant reminder of the risks he took, felt heavier with each passing hour.

Sophie, observing his unease, approached him again during a brief break. "Tesean, you don't have to keep working if it's making you this anxious. Maybe you should go back to your cell for the day," she suggested, her concern deepening.

Tesean hesitated, torn between the desire to maintain a semblance of normalcy through his work and the fear that the guards might seize the opportunity to conduct another search. "I don't want to draw attention to myself by leaving work early. The guards might find it suspicious," he replied, glancing around cautiously.

Sophie placed a hand on his arm, her gaze earnest. "Your well-being is more important than appearances, Tesean. If you're this scared, it's not worth the risk. Besides, sometimes guards double back when they know inmates are away from their cells. I don't want you to take unnecessary chances."

Her words resonated with Tesean, and he realized the truth in her advice. The fear of potential repercussions overshadowed his ability to focus on his work, and the looming uncertainty of another surprise search weighed heavily on his mind.

With a reluctant nod, he returned to his cell for the rest of the day.

As he walked back through the familiar prison corridors, the oppressive atmosphere intensified. The clanging of cell doors, the distant echoes of conversations, and the occasional footsteps of guards all served as a disturbing reminder of the confined world he navigated.

Back in his cell, Tesean closed the door with a sense of relief. The small space, while confining, offered a degree of privacy and control that felt elusive in the broader prison environment. He took a deep breath, the tension in his shoulders slowly releasing as he settled onto his bunk.

The hidden phone beckoned to him from its secret location, a silent promise of connection in the midst of isolation. Tesean hesitated, contemplating the risks and the toll this covert communication took on his mental well-being. The knowledge that he could reach out to Sophie brought comfort, yet the constant fear of discovery cast a shadow over the solace he sought.

Throughout the remainder of the day, Tesean wrestled with conflicting emotions. The fear of being caught, the desire for connection, and the practical need for a safe means of communication all vied for dominance in his thoughts. Once a refuge, the cell now felt like a battleground where the stakes were high and the cost of losing was too great.

As evening descended upon the prison, Tesean's mind remained consumed by the day's events. The routine check-ins, the whispered conversations with Sophie, and the persistent fear of exposure had left him emotionally drained. The hidden phone, no longer a source of solace, became a symbol of the intricate web of challenges he faced within the confines of his incarceration.

Nightfall brought with it a renewed sense of vulnerability. As Tesean laid on his bunk, the dim glow of the overhead light cast elongated shadows, and the uncertainty of what lied ahead lingered in the air. The fear of another surprise search, the anxiety of potential discovery, and the longing for a connection beyond prison walls merged into a disconcerting symphony.

As the prison settled into the night's stillness, Tesean couldn't escape the relentless anticipation of what the following days might bring. The hidden phone, now both a lifeline and a liability, symbolized the delicate dance he performed between the desire for connection and the ever-present shadows of uncertainty within the prison walls.

Chapter 19

Several weeks had passed since the close call that left Tesean on edge, fearing the discovery of his illicit cell phone. The routine of prison life had settled back into a semblance of normalcy, and Tesean found solace in the familiar rhythm of his daily activities. The threat of surprise searches still loomed, but the urgency of the previous weeks had faded, giving him a momentary reprieve.

Back in the prison library, Tesean resumed his role, surrounded by the comforting scent of aged books and the muted hum of activity. The shelves stood as silent witnesses to the stories they held, a stark contrast to the covert secrets hidden within the prison's walls. Tesean navigated the narrow aisles, his movements purposeful as he organized and cataloged the books.

Sophie, ever a welcomed presence, joined him in the library as part of her assigned tasks within the prison. Their bond had deepened in the wake of the shared anxieties and close encounters, creating an unspoken understanding that transcended the confines of their circumstances.

Once laced with the tension of secrecy, their interactions evolved into moments of intimacy as they found solace in each other's company. With its serene ambiance and the scent of aging paper, the library became a haven where they could momentarily escape the harsh realities of prison life.

During their shared shifts, Tesean and Sophie developed a silent language, exchanging glances and subtle gestures that conveyed more than words ever could. With its shelves of knowledge and stories, the library bore witness to the unspoken connection that flourished between them. She asked him to come into the back room with her to put some books up. Once in the room, she pushed him back onto the wall and started to pull down his pants. Once she had them where she wanted them around his thighs, she raised her shirt and tugged at her pants so that she could pull them down.

Once they were pulled down, in one swift motion, she bent over and spread her ass cheeks so that he could enter her from behind. Tesean was in heaven because this was all he had been dreaming about since they met. Since they couldn't make love due to the fear of getting caught, he grabbed her by the waist and started giving her short and quick pumps. Tesean fucked her so hard from behind that he was on the verge of a nut within a matter of minutes.

Although their session was quick, he felt this connection had just taken their relationship to another level. After emptying his load deep in her pussy they cleaned themselves up and then headed back out to finish their work day.

As the sun dipped below the prison walls, casting a warm glow through the library's tiny windows, Tesean and Sophie found themselves drawn to the quiet corners of the space. The moments between tasks became opportunities for stolen glances, lingering touches, and conversations that strayed beyond the confines of library duties.

In the gentle cadence of their exchanges, Tesean and Sophie discovered a refuge from the harsh realities surrounding them. Once a place of solitude, the library became a sanctuary where they could share stolen moments of normalcy amid the restrictive environment.

Outside the library's embrace, the nights in prison held a different kind of connection. The soft glow of the illicit cell phone illuminated the darkness of Tesean's cell as he exchanged messages with Sophie. Initially born out of the need for connection, the intimate text exchanges had taken on a more personal and sensual tone.

In the quiet night hours, when the prison slept, Tesean and Sophie engaged in different intimacy through the written word. The limitations of their physical separation melted away as they shared fantasies, whispered confessions, and the raw vulnerability of their desires.

The words on the screen carried the weight of unspoken emotions, creating a bridge that spanned the distance between their prison cells. The clandestine nature of their communication added an element of risk, heightening the intensity of each exchange. Tesean, in those stolen moments, felt a surge of connection that transcended the confines of his physical reality.

The dichotomy between the mundane routine of library shifts and the clandestine intimacy of their nighttime conversations became the pillars of Tesean's existence. With its shelves of knowledge and the comforting presence of Sophie, the library offered moments of solace and connection. The cell phone, a forbidden conduit to the outside world, became a lifeline that transcended the physical barriers of prison life.

Despite the risks, Tesean navigated the delicate balance between the desire for connection and the fear of exposure. The library became a space where he could momentarily escape the constraints of his reality, where the exchange of glances and shared smiles served as a balm for the soul.

The passing weeks brought a paradoxical sense of both closeness and separation. The physical distance between Tesean and Sophie seemed insurmountable, yet the emotional connection they forged in the quiet moments spoke of a bond that defied the limitations of their surroundings.

In the quiet hours of the night, Tesean would find himself

lying on his bunk, the soft glow of the phone casting a warm light on his face. The rhythmic exchange of messages with Sophie became a ritual that transcended the isolation of his cell, creating a world where their shared dreams and desires took precedence over the harsh realities that awaited outside.

As the days turned into weeks, the clandestine nature of their connection added a layer of thrill to their exchanges. The library, with its timeless books and muted whispers, became a backdrop to the unfolding drama of their secret bond. The cell phone, concealed within the confines of Tesean's belongings, became a source of risk and a symbol of the connection they fought to preserve.

Yet, amid the stolen moments and whispered confessions, a growing awareness of the potential consequences lingered. The fear of discovery, once a distant threat, began to cast a more prominent shadow. Tesean, entangled in the complexities of his clandestine communication, couldn't shake the nagging apprehension that the walls, with their silent watchfulness, held the secrets of his forbidden connection.

As Tesean and Sophie navigated the delicate dance of intimacy within the confines of a prison, the passing weeks brought both a deepening bond and an undercurrent of uncertainty. With its books of wisdom and tales of escapism, the library witnessed the intertwined fates of two souls seeking solace amid the shadows of incarceration.

Chapter 20

In the quiet corners of the library, where the hushed whispers of turning pages mingled with the soft rustling of paper, Tesean found the courage to express feelings that had long been tucked away in the recesses of his heart. Sophie engrossed in a book, looked up as Tesean approached, his footsteps echoing in the library's serene atmosphere.

He cleared his throat, nervously adjusting the collar of his shirt. Tesean and Sophie had been colleagues for months, working in the same office building. Their desks were situated not far from each other, yet the invisible barrier of unspoken words had kept them from acknowledging the growing connection between them.

"Sophie," Tesean began, his eyes locked onto hers, "there's something I need to tell you."

Sophie closed her book, her curiosity piqued. "Sure, Tesean. What's on your mind?"

Tesean took a deep breath, gathering his thoughts. "I've been trying to find the right words, but it's difficult. You mean a lot to me, Sophie. More than just a coworker. I've been grappling with these feelings for a while now, and I can't keep them hidden any longer."

Sophie studied Tesean's face, sensing the sincerity in his words. "What is it, Tesean? You can tell me anything."

Tesean took another breath, his gaze unwavering. "Sophie, I'm in love with you."

The admission hung in the air, creating a momentary silence stretching into eternity. Sophie's eyes widened in surprise, and a warmth spread across her face, transforming into a soft smile. Tesean's heart raced, unsure of how she would respond.

"Sophie," he continued, "I've tried to fight it, to ignore these feelings, but I can't. You've become a beacon of light in my life, and I can't imagine my days without you."

Sophie's smile widened, and she gently touched Tesean's arm. "Tesean, I've been feeling the same way. I didn't know how to say it."

Relief washed over Tesean as he realized the depth of their connection. The weight of unspoken emotions lifted, creating a newfound sense of openness. Once a silent witness to their unexpressed feelings, the library became the backdrop for a pivotal moment in their lives.

With a shared understanding, Tesean and Sophie decided to take the next step. They embraced the joy of being in each other's company, allowing their relationship to blossom into something beautiful and genuine.

Their connection deepened as days turned into weeks and weeks into months. They navigated the challenges of building a relationship within the confines of the workplace, cherishing stolen moments in the library where it all began.

However, their journey faced an unexpected hurdle. Tesean, unbeknownst to many, had a past that he had been trying to overcome. The specter of a prison sentence loomed over him, a consequence of mistakes made in his youth. Despite the challenges, Sophie stood by him, unwavering in her support.

The couple embarked on creating a home filled with love and understanding. Together, they faced the challenges of blending their lives and forging a path toward a shared future. The library, where their love story began, remained a cherished memory—a reminder of the courage it took to express their feelings and the strength of their bond.

As they planned their life together, Tesean and Sophie discovered the transformative power of love. This force could overcome obstacles, heal wounds, and create a haven of happiness amid life's uncertainties. Their commitment to each other became a testament to the enduring nature of love, proving that even the quiet corners of a library could hold the key to a lifetime of shared dreams and love.

Chapter 21

The prison gates clanged shut behind Tesean as he returned to his cell. Today was different; there was a newfound lightness in his step, a smile that seemed to refuse to leave his face. He had finally mustered the courage to express his feelings to Sophie, and she, in turn, reciprocated, making their relationship official. The weight burdened Tesean for so long now felt lifted, replaced by the warmth of shared affection.

As he approached his cell, Tesean couldn't help but feel a sense of anticipation. The familiar routine of returning to his confined space after a day's work held a new significance today. With every step, he replayed the joyous moments he had shared with Sophie, the promises of a future together echoing in his mind.

However, as he pushed open the metal door and entered the dimly lit cell, his joy was abruptly replaced by confusion and a tinge of anxiety. Tyson, his cellmate, was sitting on Tesean's bunk, an unfamiliar expression on his face. In his hands, he held Tesean's cell phone.

Tesean's heart sank as he saw Tyson examining the phone. "Tyson, what are you doing with my phone?" he asked, a knot of worry forming in his stomach.

Tyson looked up, seemingly surprised. "Hey, Tesean. I found this on your bed when I came back from the yard. Thought I'd keep it safe for you."

Tesean's initial confusion morphed into frustration. He reached out and grabbed the phone from Tyson's hands, his voice tinged with irritation. "You can't just go through my stuff, man. Where did you get this?"

Tyson raised his hands defensively, his tone apologetic. "Easy, Tesean. I didn't mean any harm. It was just lying there, and I didn't want someone else getting their hands on it."

Tesean took a deep breath, trying to calm the sudden surge of anger. He couldn't afford trouble in prison, especially now that he had something to lose. "Look, Tyson, I appreciate your concern, but you can't take things without asking. This is mine. I need to know where you found it."

Tyson scratched his head, looking genuinely perplexed. "I told you, man. It was on your bed when I came in."

As Tesean processed Tyson's words, a realization dawned on him. He vividly remembered leaving his phone on the bed this morning, but now he questioned why he had done that. He couldn't recall ever being so careless with his belongings.

His frustration turned inward, and he sighed, acknowledging the possibility that he might have been the cause of this misunderstanding. "Tyson, I'm sorry for snapping at you. I should have been more careful with my things. It's just... this phone is important to me.

Tyson nodded understandingly, his earlier concern turning into a lighthearted grin. "No worries, Tesean. I get it. You gotta be careful in here."

Tesean hesitated momentarily, contemplating whether to share the truth with Tyson. He knew the risks of having a phone in prison—strict rules and severe consequences. Yet, a newfound sense of trust and camaraderie urged him to confide in his cellmate.

"Tyson, this phone, it's not supposed to be here. I couldn't tell anyone about it because it could get us both in trouble. I appreciate your understanding, but we must be discreet about this, okay?"

Tyson's eyes widened, a mix of surprise and curiosity dancing in them. "Seriously? How'd you manage to get a phone in here?"

Tesean leaned in, his voice lowered to a whisper. "Let's just say I've got my ways. But we need to keep it between us. The last thing we want is the guards finding out."

Tyson nodded solemnly, the weight of the secret settling between them. In that dimly lit cell, an unspoken pact formed

—a bond of trust that transcended the confines of their prison walls.

As Tesean settled onto his bunk, the glow of his earlier happiness faded, replaced by a new awareness of the delicate balance he now had to maintain. The cell phone, a forbidden yet precious connection to the outside world, symbolized the risks he was willing to take for love and the newfound understanding between him and Tyson.

In the confines of their shared space, Tesean and Tyson navigated the complexities of prison life, their connection deepening as they faced the challenges ahead. The library, where Tesean had once found the courage to express his love for Sophie, now seemed like a distant memory. Yet, in the quiet moments of their shared existence, the library's influence lingered—a reminder that even within the harsh realities of prison, unexpected connections could emerge, bringing with them the promise of understanding and a shared journey toward an uncertain but hopeful future.

THE DIM GLOW of the prison cell's solitary lightbulb cast a soft, muted illumination across the small space. Tesean laid on his bunk, the day's events replaying in his mind like a relentless loop. The unsettling encounter replaced the thrill of officially being in a relationship with Sophie with Tesean and realizing the potential risks he faced.

Tesean pulled out his contraband cell phone, glancing at the screen. The faint glow illuminated his face as he composed a message to Sophie. He needed to share the day's events with her, to unburden his thoughts and seek solace in her understanding.

"Hey Sophie," he typed, "something happened today. Tyson found my phone, and I had to explain. It's all good now, but I just wanted to let you know. I promise I'll be more careful from now on."

As Tesean sent the message, he felt a mixture of relief and anxiety. The clandestine nature of their communication added an extra layer of complexity to their relationship, requiring constant vigilance. The vulnerability of their connection hung in the air, and Tesean anxiously awaited Sophie's response.

Minutes felt like hours as he stared at the phone, his thoughts drifting between the consequences of the day's events and the warmth of Sophie's understanding. Finally, a message popped on the screen, and he eagerly opened it.

"Hey Tesean," Sophie's words appeared, a digital lifeline from the outside world. "I'm glad you're okay. Just be more careful with the phone, alright? We can't afford any slip-ups. I love you, and I believe in you. Stay strong."

Tesean exhaled, a mixture of gratitude and love swelling within him. Sophie's support provided the reassurance he needed, a reminder that they were in this together despite their physical distance and challenges.

"Thanks, Sophie," he typed back, his fingers dancing

across the tiny keypad. "I'll be more careful, I promise. Love you too. Goodnight."

With a sense of resolution, Tesean tucked the phone away, vowing to be more cautious. The weight of responsibility settled on his shoulders, a reminder of the delicate balance he needed to maintain in the confines of his cell.

As he laid back on his bunk, the prison's nighttime routine echoed around him—the distant shuffle of inmates, the occasional clang of metal against metal. The solitude of the cell became both a sanctuary and a prison within a prison, where emotions were amplified, and secrets were guarded with utmost care.

In the quiet moments before sleep claimed him, Tesean reflected on the complexities of his reality. The forbidden phone, a lifeline to the world beyond the prison walls, symbolized his lengths to nurture his connection with Sophie. Their relationship, born in the shadows of secrecy, faced the challenges of an environment that demanded constant vigilance.

With Sophie's words echoing, Tesean drifted into a restless slumber. The dreams that danced on the edge of his consciousness were tinged with a determination to navigate the intricacies of love within the confines of a place designed to extinguish it.

Morning light filtered through the narrow window, casting a new day into the cell. Tesean woke with a renewed sense of purpose. As he prepared for another day in the harsh reality of prison life, he carried with him the weight of responsibility and the promise he had made to Sophie—to be more careful, to guard their connection, and to face the challenges ahead with unwavering resolve.

The library, where he had first found the courage to express his love, felt like a distant memory. Yet, in the quiet moments of the night, the echoes of Sophie's support and the digital glow of their forbidden communication served as a reminder that love, even in the most challenging circumstances, could endure. And so, Tesean faced the day with a newfound determination, knowing that every careful step he took was a testament to the strength of the bond he shared with Sophie—a bond that transcended the confines of his prison cell and held the promise of a future beyond the walls that sought to confine them.

Chapter 22

The prison yard stretched out before Tesean, a barren expanse enclosed by towering fences topped with razor wire. The air was heavy with the scent of confinement, but Tesean welcomed the opportunity to step outside, if only for a brief respite from the monotony of prison life. It had been a long time since he had taken advantage of the yard for a workout, and today seemed like the perfect day to do so.

Dressed in his standard-issue prison uniform, Tesean went to the makeshift outdoor gym area. The clang of metal weights and the grunts of inmates engaged in physical exertion filled the air. As he approached, some familiar faces greeted him with nods and smiles, recognizing him from the sporadic times he had joined their workout sessions.

"Hey, Tesean! Where have you been, man?" called out Marcus, a burly inmate with a shaved head and a perpetual scowl.

Tesean gave a half-smile in return, a mix of guilt and evasion. "Hey, Marcus. Just been busy, you know? Work's been exhausting lately."

Marcus raised an eyebrow, skeptical. "Exhausting? You used to be a regular out here. What changed?"

Tesean hesitated, searching for an explanation that wouldn't reveal his valid reasons. The truth—that he had been working in the library to be close to Sophie—was a secret he couldn't risk sharing. The prison grapevine was notorious for spreading information faster than wildfire.

"Just been tired, man," Tesean replied with a nonchalant shrug. "Library duty takes a lot out of me. I want to crash in my cell once I'm done."

His friends exchanged knowing glances, a silent acknowledgment that life behind bars could indeed take its toll. Marcus clapped Tesean on the back, a gesture of camaraderie. "I get it, bro. We all need our rest. But don't be a stranger. You're one of the crew."

Tesean nodded appreciatively, grateful for the understanding of his fellow inmates. As he joined the workout, the rhythmic clinks of weights and the grunts of exertion drowned out his inner thoughts. The physical activity provided a temporary escape, a way to channel the frustrations and complexities of prison life into something tangible and controlled.

Amid the makeshift gym, Tesean felt a sense of belonging. The camaraderie forged through shared struggles and shared moments of respite offered a semblance of normalcy in the otherwise rigid confines of the prison environment.

As the workout continued, Tesean's mind drifted back to the library, to the moments spent with Sophie amid the hushed whispers of turning pages. The secret nature of their connection weighed on him, creating a delicate dance between the desire to share his joy with his friends and the need to protect the fragile reality he had built.

After the workout, as Tesean wiped the sweat from his brow, Marcus approached him once more. "Seriously, Tesean, if you ever need anything, we got your back. You're not alone in this place."

Tesean nodded, touched by the sincerity of Marcus' words. With its unforgiving fences and towering walls, the yard seemed less imposing in the face of the genuine connections he had forged within it.

Later that evening, as Tesean settled into his cell, the weight of secrecy lingered. The library, the yard, and the daily interactions became part of a complex dance he performed to maintain the delicate balance between his newfound happiness with Sophie and the realities of prison life.

He pulled out his contraband cell phone, a forbidden lifeline to the outside world. The library, where it all began, held the key to their connection—which required constant vigilance and discretion.

As Tesean texted Sophie about his day, he couldn't shake the feeling that he was navigating two worlds—the confined and regimented space of prison and the vast, boundless realm of emotions and possibilities beyond its walls.

"Workout today. Missed being out there with the guys," he typed, offering a glimpse into his day without revealing too much.

Sophie's response was quick and understanding. "Take care of yourself, Tesean. We'll figure this out together. Love you."

As Tesean settled into the rhythm of prison life, he carried with him the support of his friends in the yard, the clandestine connection with Sophie, and the promise of a future that transcended the confines of his cell. Once a sanctuary of quiet moments with Sophie, the library now symbolized resilience and hope—a place where love persisted in the face of adversity.

In the dim light of the cell, Tesean closed his eyes, reflecting on the complexities of his reality. The library, the yard, and the forbidden phone were threads in the intricate tapestry of his life behind bars. As he drifted into sleep, he clung to the promise he had made to Sophie, vowing to navigate the challenges of prison life with unwavering determination and the enduring strength of their connection.

THE PRISON CAFETERIA buzzed with the murmur of inmates in various stages of morning wakefulness. Tesean stood in line, tray in hand, waiting for his turn to receive a meager breakfast. The air was thick with the scent of institutional food, and the clatter of trays and cutlery created a chaotic symphony.

As he inched forward in line, Tesean couldn't help but feel a familiar sense of routine settling over him. The morning rituals of the prison—breakfast, headcount, and the beginning of another day—had become a monotonous backdrop to his life behind bars.

His thoughts, however, were far from routine. The events of the previous day lingered in his mind—the workout in the yard, the clandestine messages with Sophie, and the delicate dance of secrecy that defined his relationship. Tesean's newfound happiness was tempered by the constant awareness of the risks of maintaining a connection beyond the prison walls.

As he neared the serving counter, a voice interrupted his thoughts. "Hey, Tesean!"

Turning, Tesean found himself face to face with Eddie, a fellow inmate he had encountered in the yard on occasion. Eddie was a stocky man with a scruffy beard, a figure that seemed to blend into the background of the prison population.

"What's up, Eddie?" Tesean replied, nodding in acknowledgment.

Eddie leancd in, lowering his voice as if sharing a secret.

"I heard you got a thing going on with one of the staff members. Is that true?"

Tesean's eyes narrowed, a mixture of surprise and frustration flashing across his face. He hadn't expected his connection with Sophie to become the subject of prison gossip so quickly. He hesitated for a moment, weighing his response carefully.

"Where did you hear that?" Tesean asked, trying to sound nonchalant.

Eddie chuckled, a sly grin spreading across his face. "Word travels fast in here, man. So, spill, is it true?"

Tesean's jaw tightened. The secrecy surrounding his relationship with Sophie was paramount, and the last thing he needed was for rumors to spread like wildfire. He took a deep breath, choosing his words with caution. "Look, Eddie, I don't know where you heard that, but nothing is happening. Just rumors, you know how it is."

Eddie raised an eyebrow, a mischievous glint in his eye. "Come on, Tesean, don't be coy. You've been spending a lot of time in the library lately. And there's a lady working there who's been catching your eye."

Tesean's frustration simmered beneath the surface. The prison grapevine, fueled by speculation and idle chatter, had a way of distorting reality. Sophie, the woman who had brought light into his life, was now the subject of dubious rumors.

"She's just a coworker, Eddie. We work in the same department, that's all," Tesean replied, his tone firm.

Eddie leaned in closer, his voice dropping to a conspiratorial whisper. "Come on, Tesean, I've been here long enough to know when someone's holding back. You think a staff member is interested in an inmate like you?"

Anger flared within Tesean, but he bit back the instinctive retort that threatened to escape. He had to tread carefully, mindful of the delicate balance between maintaining his privacy and deflecting Eddie's probing questions.

"She's not like the others," Tesean said, his voice edged with a controlled frustration. "She's different. Just doing her job, you know?"

Eddie chuckled dismissively, unwilling to accept Tesean's explanation. "Yeah, right. I'll believe it when I see it. Staff members don't get involved with inmates, man."

Tesean's grip tightened on his tray, his jaw clenching in response to Eddie's skepticism. He knew the risks of revealing the truth, of acknowledging the depth of his connection with Sophie. The prison environment was unforgiving, and any hint of impropriety could have severe consequences.

"You can believe what you want, Eddie," Tesean replied, forcing a calm demeanor. "But she's not like the others. Just drop it."

Sensing the tension in Tesean's demeanor, Eddie decided to back away from the conversation. "Alright, man, if you say so. Just don't let it get you in trouble."

As Eddie retreated, Tesean exhaled a sigh of relief. The encounter was a stark reminder of the delicate dance he had to perform within the prison's confined space. The secrecy of his relationship with Sophie was both a source of joy and a burden that required constant vigilance and the ability to deflect prying eyes and probing questions.

With his tray in hand, Tesean moved toward an empty table, the din of the cafeteria fading into the background. As he sat down, he reflected on the challenges of maintaining a connection that defied the rigid boundaries of prison life.

Later that day, as he returned to the library, the quiet sanctuary where his connection with Sophie had blossomed, Tesean couldn't shake the unease from his encounter with Eddie. The library's shelves, filled with books and the whispers of shared moments, offered a brief respite from the complexities of his reality.

As he worked among the quiet aisles, Tesean pondered the intricacies of his relationship with Sophie. Their connection, born in secrecy, faced the constant threat of exposure. The library, once a refuge from the noise of prison life, now served as a place where he sought solace and reaffirmed the promise he had made—to protect their connection at all costs.

In the quiet moments between bookshelves, Tesean vowed to navigate the challenges ahead with resilience and determination. With its silent presence, the library became a symbol of hope—a place where love persisted, even in the face of doubt and skepticism within the prison's confined world. And so, Tesean pressed on, embracing the clandestine nature of his connection and finding strength in the whispers of shared moments that transcended the boundaries of his prison cell.

Chapter 23

The library, a haven of quiet and solitude, had always been a sanctuary for Tesean. Its shelves lined with books, the soft hum of fluorescent lights, and the occasional rustle of pages provided a respite from the harsh realities of prison life. However, on this particular day, the library offered no solace as the weight of rumors hung in the air.

Tesean sat at the library desk, distracted by the murmurs and hushed conversations that seemed to follow him like shadows. The air in the library felt stifling, and the usually comforting atmosphere now bore the weight of the secrets he and Sophie shared.

He overheard snippets of conversations from other

inmates, the speculative whispers that had somehow found their way into the quiet corners of the library. The rumors about him and Sophie spread like wildfire, threatening the delicate balance they had tried to maintain.

Tesean couldn't shake the sense of unease that settled in the pit of his stomach. Once a refuge, the library now felt like a place of scrutiny. Every glance from fellow inmates seemed laden with questions, and the whispers that reached his ears threatened to unravel the carefully guarded secret of his connection with Sophie.

The need to protect Sophie, to shield her from the potential consequences of their clandestine relationship, weighed heavily on Tesean's mind. He knew that if the rumors gained traction and reached the ears of the prison staff, both he and Sophie could face serious repercussions.

After another discreet glance over his shoulder, Tesean decided it was time to address the issue. He discreetly pulled out his contraband cell phone and sent a message to Sophie.

"Hey, Sophie, we need to talk. Meet me in the usual spot during our break."

Sophie, who had been diligently shelving books, looked up at the notification on her phone. Concern etched her features as she excused herself from her duties and went to the designated spot where they often shared stolen moments during their breaks.

As Tesean awaited Sophie's arrival, he felt a mix of

anxiety and determination. With its muted ambiance, the library seemed to echo with the weight of unspoken conversations. Sophie joined him, her eyes searching his face for answers.

"Tesean, what's going on?" Sophie asked, her voice filled with concern.

Tesean took a deep breath, choosing his words carefully. "Sophie, it's about the rumors. People are talking, and I'm worried it might get out of hand. I overheard inmates discussing us, and we need to be cautious."

Sophie's brows furrowed, frustration and worry crossing her features. "Tesean, we've been careful. How did this happen?"

Tesean shook his head, a sense of responsibility heavy on his shoulders. "I don't know, but we need to address it. If the rumors spread, it could put both of us in jeopardy. I can't let that happen to you."

Sophie sighed, realizing the gravity of the situation. "But, Tesean, we've been careful. We can't control what others say."

"I know, Sophie," Tesean replied, his gaze filled with determination. "But we can control our actions. We need to cut back on talking while we're at work. It's the only way to minimize the risk."

Sophie's expression shifted, a mix of disappointment and understanding. "Tesean, I don't like it, but I understand the necessity. It's just frustrating that we have to be so cautious."

Tesean reached out to gently hold Sophie's hand. "I know,

Sophie, and I hate that it has to be like this. But we need to protect each other. We'll find other moments, other places to be together. It's just temporary."

Sophie nodded reluctantly, the weight of the situation settling in. "Okay, Tesean. I trust you and don't want anything bad to happen to either of us."

As they stood hand in hand, the reality of their secret love became even more apparent. Once a refuge, the library had transformed into a place of tension and caution. Yet, in that moment, Tesean and Sophie forged a silent pact—an agreement to navigate the challenges ahead with resilience and determination.

In the days that followed, Tesean and Sophie adhered to their decision. The library became a place of restraint, the stolen glances and shared moments replaced by the silent acknowledgment of their commitment to each other's safety.

As they found new spots and quiet corners within the prison to steal moments away from prying eyes, Tesean and Sophie clung to the hope that one day their love wouldn't need to be hidden, that the shadows of secrecy would finally give way to the light of freedom.

He longed for the day he could place soft, wet kisses along her neck. Tesean wished that he could run his hands up the side of her body and up to her breasts. He wanted to squeeze her voluptuous mounds firmly, loving how soft the flesh felt between his fingers.

The first chance he got, Tesean planned to place kisses down her neck and chest until his lips met her erect nipples.

He wanted Sophie to moan softly as he explored her body. He wanted her reaction to let him know she loved how he switched his attention between each breast, giving them the attention they were begging for.

He knew then that he had her just where he wanted her, just how he wanted her.

In one quick motion, Tesean let go of her breast and moved a hand to her pussy so that he could rub on her clit with his thumb.

Just as Sophie began to moan his name, his dick strained painfully in his underwear as he stuck two fingers into her. Her pussy was so wet and slick as her pussy muscles gripped his thick fingers tightly. Curling his fingers deeper into her wetness, he lifted his head so that he could meet her eyes. Sophie was the most beautiful woman he had ever seen, and he was so thankful to see her so vulnerable as he brought her pleasure. He could tell that she wanted this just as bad as he did.

He could feel her starting to tense up and knew that she was on the verge of cumming.

"Relax, love," he mumbled as he brought his lips to hers and pressed his thumb to her clit again, applying delicious pressure.

During one of their many late-night conversations, he remembered that she had a bad habit of tensing up right before she came, so he reminded her to relax. Tesean had read that orgasms were much more intense and pleasurable when the body was free of tension; he wanted her to have the best that she had ever had at this moment. He wanted to please and make her feel good in every way possible.

He was satisfied when he felt her body relax under him.

Before she reached her peak, Tesean was awakened by one of the guards yelling for him to get up. It was time for him to go back to population. He had just completed ninety days in solitary confinement for damn near beating another inmate to sleep.

He sat on the edge of his bed and looked around the dark cell, only to realize that his entire experience with the librarian was a figment of his imagination. Tesean was far from the model inmate, and there was no way he would ever get the privilege of working in the prison's library or for any other job in the prison.

THE END

Did you enjoy the read?
Let us know how much by leaving us a review on Amazon
and Goodreads.

. . .

Keep reading for a preview of…

Wet Dreams On Lockdown:
The Nurse
By Elijah R. Freeman

CHAPTER 1

"Ow! Goddamn, bitch! Why you squeezing it so hard? That shit hurts!"

Dominique sighed as she squeezed the inmate's eyebrows together to stop the bleeding. The prison nurse was frustrated with the inmate that she was helping.

He was a scrawny, black male who she was sure was on drugs, tweaking out. Somehow, he had gotten his eyebrow slit open and she needed to get the bleeding under control so she could see if he would need stitches or not.

"I'm sorry, Mr. Kemp, but I have to get this bleeding under control so I can determine how deep it is. I know it doesn't feel good, but I need you to bear with me. I'll be able to get you some pain meds after."

"Pain meds? What kind of meds?"

Dominique had to resist the urge to roll her eyes when he

125

perked up at the mention of pain meds. His reaction had confirmed her suspicions. He was a drug addict looking for a fix, which was more than likely the reason he ended up in the nurses' office in the first place.

"Tylenol. Now sit still, please," she said dismissively.

The man mumbled something under his breath but sat still. Every once in a while, he would wince when she applied pressure to his brow, to see if the bleeding had stopped.

Dominique held her breath, only breathing through her mouth while she patched the man up because the stench that rolled off of him was so foul, that she struggled not to gag. Further validating her thoughts that his visit to her was drug-related. It was common for inmates to sell their hygiene products and rarely shower.

Ten minutes later, she applied petroleum jelly to his brow and put a Band-Aid over it. "Alright, Mr. Kemp. You're all patched up." Turning around, she walked over to a cupboard, grabbed a bottle of Tylenol and a small plastic cup, dropped two tablets into it, then handed it to him. "Take these, and the guard will go ahead and escort you back to your dorm."

"Thank you, beautiful." The inmate said as he hopped off of the medical table.

Dominique knocked on the office door and it opened up right away. The C.O. standing on the other side gestured for the man to come out.

Dominique didn't respond to the man as he walked out of the room. Once the officer that was standing outside of the door closed it behind them, she rolled her eyes. Getting called things like "beautiful," "sexy," and "gorgeous" after being cussed out for attempting to help the injured or sickly inmates wasn't anything new. She was used to it for the most part. None of the compliments that she got from any of them flattered her. She always assumed that it was just jail talk, anyway. Many of the inmates had been locked up for long periods of time, so naturally, most of them that came to her office were able to appreciate her natural beauty.

Dominique was a full-figured, five-foot-seven. The middle part of her name had earned her the nickname, Mini, but she was far from that. A plus-size woman, she had ample breast, thick thighs and a nice, plump ass, something she couldn't hide under her scrubs. Her mahogany skin was flawless, showing that she took good care of herself and had a high water intake. She had a pretty face, free of any traces of make-up, allowing her natural beauty to shine through daily.

The sound of a familiar and rhythmic knock at the door, caught her attention. "Come in!" She ripped off the disposable paper on the medical table, in preparation for the next patient. Grabbing a can of Lysol, she sprayed and wiped the faux leather material down before covering it with more paper.

"You good, girl?" Her best friend and co-worker Sierra asked as walked in. Sierra was a Correctional Officer there at Valdosta State Prison. The two had been childhood best friends and they loved being able to work together.

"Yeah, why you ask that?" Dominique turned around to

look at her friend. The worry that she heard in her voice threw her for a loop.

"I was just making sure. That nigga that just left outta here is a weirdo. Got his head busted 'cause he don't pay his debts. I just got done talkin' to my lil boo and he let me know what was going on. I just wanted to check on you and make sure that junkie wasn't bothering you. I'll have his ass jumped on again if he tried you." Sierra pulled the large band holding her braids together in a bun, letting them cascade down her back.

Dominique gave her friend a disapproving look. "Well, I'm fine, so don't feel the need to have nobody jumped on my behalf." She shook her head as she went to a cupboard and used a set of keys to unlock it so she could access the supply of hypodermic needles and insulin. The next inmate that was due to see her was a diabetic that would need his insulin shot. "I see you still fuckin' around with these inmates. You ain't learn yo lesson last time?"

Sierra rolled her eyes at Dominique's concern as she worked to put her braids back in a bun. They had been too tight and were giving her a headache. With six hours left on her shift, the relief was much needed. "You so boring. Instead of worrying about me, *you* should have a little fun and find one of these niggas to fuck wit', too. Some of these niggas in here got long dick *and* money. Make this shit work for you, girl! You workin' *two* jobs when you could just work here and get in good with one of these bosses in here."

Once Sierra was done re-doing her hair, she put her hands

on her hips and watched Dominique maneuver around the room. After preparing the necessary supplies that she would need to tend to her next patient, she sat at the computer to document what she had done for Mr. Kemp. Documentation was necessary. If there was no record, it didn't happen. Each inmate was required to pay a five-dollar co-pay fee whenever they visited medical, and the medical supervisor did not play about them co-pays. Dominique didn't have the time or patience for a lecture

"I don't know. I've thought about it, but I don't wanna lose my license. I worked too hard and am in too much debt to risk it messing around with a criminal." She said as she began typing on the computer.

"There you go being judgmental and shit. Just 'cause niggas are criminals and in prison doesn't mean they're bad people. I mean, shit, you know that *I* do what I do 'cause I have to. I have kids to feed, and I don't have time to go out and date because I work so much. This is all convenient for me. It could be convenient for you, too. Hell, you *need* some dick. Maybe then you wouldn't be so uptight."

Sierra had been urging her friend to "have fun" with some of the inmates while making some extra cash in the process for the last three months. The idea had never been something that settled right with Dominique, but at times she did feel tempted. Of the two friends, she was the good girl, always aiming to do the right thing and remain on the right side of the law.

But Dominique's thoughts often wandered into the forbidden territory that Sierra so casually inhabited. She could almost taste the thrill of the unknown, the allure of quick money, and the rush of stepping outside her own meticulously drawn lines. Every time Sierra shared her tales of excitement and gain, something in Dominique's chest tightened—a mix of fear, lust, and curiosity.

At night, alone with her thoughts, Dominique would sometimes catch herself crafting scenarios in her mind where she crossed that invisible line, just to feel the adrenaline of the *what if.* She had even strummed her clit a few times to prison nurse porn. Yet she clung to her principles like a life raft, reminding herself of the consequences, the betrayal of her values, and the disappointment of those she loved.

Even when Sierra pointed out the seemingly harmless nature of it all, or how easy it was, Dominique found herself wet with need, her face a well-rehearsed mask hiding her internal conflict. She was teetering on a precipice, drawn by the siren call of temptation, yet every time she peered over the edge, her heart recoiled, and she stepped back, reaffirming her resolve.

The truth was, Dominique wanted to try it, to break free from her restraints, if only for a moment, but she couldn't—wouldn't—admit it.

So she remained the good girl, the anchor in the storm of Sierra's schemes, quietly patching the cracks in her armor and hoping that, with time, the temptation would fade into a distant memory, never to be realized. Dominique understood the stakes were high, and the cost of losing herself in the depths of that enticing darkness was far too great. There was, after all, no turning back from some choices, and she wasn't willing to gamble with the life she had so carefully built.

"Are you done?" Dominique asked, typing away at the computer.

"Fuck you, bitch. Fine... one day yo ass gonna see what I'm talking about. All it's gonna take is the right nigga to walk in this office and it'll be a wrap. Watch."

Dominique looked over her shoulder to see Sierra's tall, slim-petite frame halfway out of the door. The woman pointed a short, baby pink painted acrylic nail at her, her pretty chocolate skin seemingly glowing from within. "I'ma getchu." Then she slipped fully out of the door, the heavy metal shutting hard behind her.

Dominique rolled her eyes, let out a heavy sigh, and shook her head before returning to the task of documenting her last visit.

A part of her was frustrated. She was extremely tired and in the middle of a twenty-four-hour shift. After completing a grueling twelve-hour shift at South Georgia Medical Center, she headed directly to the prison to endure another eight-hour stint. Once her duties there concluded, she would be granted a mere two hours of rest before returning to the hospital for an additional four hours of work. To say she was exhausted would be an understatement.

As she worked, her best friend's words were repeating over and over in her head. It was true that she worked so long and hard that she barely even had time for herself, let alone a man. She often felt lonely, intimacy and affection being things that she craved but was virtually impossible thanks to the fact that she had to work so much. While Sierra hadn't been wrong, the risk seemed far greater than the reward.

Plus, there hadn't been one inmate that came into her office that she had been even slightly attracted to. None of them were her type and none of them she found worthy of giving her pussy up to.

Fucking with an inmate at Valdosta State Prison was out.

"Ain't no mufuckin' way, bruh. I know I'm not trippin'! My shit was in my box and now it's not. Where the fuck is my shit?"

Ramello shook his head as he sat on his cot, texting on his cell phone. Nine other Muslims were present in the cell as well, posted up arms folded or standing about except for Badazz, who was tweaking out because his phone and some of his work had gone missing from his locker box. Around him in the tight space of Ramello's cell, the Muslims had gathered to figure out what was going on.

Earlier, Badazz had rushed out of his cell to catch a play at the door and threw his stuff on the bottom shelf under some clothes. On his way back, he was stopped by someone on the wall phone who needed his Cash App while he had his people on the line. The dorm officer, who he was cool with, called his name to help grab the ice cooler for the dorm at the front gate, so he assisted and now his property was missing.

Ramello looked up to see the man's anger written all over his face. The vein in his neck stood out, thick and prominent, as he yelled, his fist slamming into his hand as he spoke each word.

"My shit ain't up and walk away by itself, bruh. Somebody in this mufucka got my shit and if it doesn't come up, I'm finna flip this bitch! I don't give a fuck if I gotta free-pick a nigga!"

Ramello scratched at the stubble of his beard and looked around the room, gauging the reaction of the eight other Muslims squeezed into his cell. It was clear that a thief was among them and needed to be weeded out.

"As-salamu-Alakum, Ahki. Calm down. We gon' figure this shit out." Jihad, an OG attempted to soothe the young hothead. "Look, they about to call Chow. Y'all all go and while y'all out, I'ma go see if anybody seen anything. Aiight?"

The older man looked young for his age, having taken good care of his body by being disciplined in his eating and workout habits. He was a level-headed man that who kept their operations running smoothly and was well respected and known to be extremely deadly. A lifer with no chance of parole, he took his job seriously. It gave him purpose.

"Nah, fuck that–"

"Come on, bruh, we ain't even about to be down there that long. Let him do what he gotta do so we can get yo shit back." Fetty, another Muslim, and one of Badazz's closest friends put a hand on his shoulder and began pushing him toward the door.

As if on cue, chow was being called.

Badazz was going to protest but stopped as the rest of his brothers began filing out of the room. He released a frustrated sigh and followed behind them.

Ramello and his bunkmate Haniyf were the only two that remained.

"Who you think did it? A lot of shit been coming up missin' lately..." Haniyf cleared his things from his bed and began putting them in one of the spots that he had a junkie build in the wall of his cell.

"Ain't no tellin'. I wish a nigga would try that shit wit' me, though. Get his ass fucked over." Ramello grabbed his knife from under his pillow and tucked it into his waistline. "You goin' to chow?"

"Hell yea, Bro. I'm hungry as a mufucka." Haniyf began sealing the spot.

"Hold up, then, nigga. If yeen goin', I need to put my shit up, too." Ramello handed Haniyf his phone, they sealed it in the spot and together they made their way to the chow hall.

Twenty minutes later, Ramello and Haniyf were walking back to their cell when they noticed that the door was slightly ajar. "The fuck?" Ramello said and snatched the door open to find a short, dirty, lanky nigga named Bart bent over searching under his mat. He looked up, and his eyes widened with fear.

"Melly!"

"The fuck!?

"Wazzam, nephew? I was just—" his eyes darted wildly around the room until they landed back on his mat. "Fixin' ya bed. Yea, fixin' ya bed for you." He reached for the covers and Ramello rushed him.

"Arggg!" Bart yelled in pain, and charged at Ramello headfirst in an attempt to defend himself.

The only thing that could be heard was the scuffling of shoes and banging against walls, bed and locker box.

"Yeah, fuck that nigga up, Melly!" Haniyf shouted as he egged Ramello on.

Ramello was in a rage, almost in disbelief that a nigga had the nerve to think it was sweet for him to come in his shit and even *attempt* to take some shit from him. The fact that he had caught him in the act only pissed him off even further. His six-foot-two frame towered over the much shorter man as he let off a barrage of punches all over the man's body.

"Oh, shit! Melly! Mell! Mell, man stop!" Ramello heard Jihad and the concerned voices of others. The urgency in their tones was muffled by the beat of his fury, causing him to barely register their presence as they rushed to see what the commotion was about.

It wasn't until two of his brothers were pulling him off of the thief that he let up. "Yeah, fuck nigga! Thought you could try that shit wit' me. I'm on yo ass every mufuckin' time I see you."

"Chill, nigga, look at yo leg! We gotta get'chu to medical. We gon' take care of him. You gotta go." Worry was evident in Jihad's voice as he tried to calm Ramello down.

Badazz stabbed Bart in the head, sending blood splattering on the wall. Fetty, Haniyf, and five more Muslims began stomping and kicking him as he balled up and screamed.

Ramello was so worked up that he hadn't noticed the big red stain on his thigh that was growing and spreading down his pants leg. It seemed as if the moment he laid eyes on the blood seeping through his white pants, a sharp pain began to shoot through his thigh.

"Man, what the fuck?!" He pulled at the large slit that went almost entirely across the width of his thigh. Pieces of pink and brown flesh peeked through the slit in his pants as blood spewed from the wound heavily. "This nigga stabbed me?" He was in disbelief.

"Officer! We need medical!" Jihad was at the dorm's door, banging on it repeatedly attempting to get the attention of the officer sitting in the booth.

Moments later, Sierra was popping the door and stepping in to see what the issue was. Her eyes widened the moment she laid eyes on Ramello and saw the large blood stain and rip in his pants. With a guy at each side of him, helping him walk, he limped towards her.

"Ms. Jones! Ms. Jones! We got one need to go to medical," one of the guys said.

Someone getting stabbed at a level 5 prison was normal, and usually wouldn't have been taken as seriously but an inmate had just died the week before due to a leg wound. He had only been stabbed once but that was all it took when you hit a major artery.

"Come on! Come on! Come on!" She frantically waved him over as she held the door open, her eyes quickly scanning the dorm looking for signs of any distress. Besides a few stray people sitting around at tables or poking their heads out of the door, she didn't notice anything out of the norm. Nothing stuck out to her immediately, so she decided not to call a code until she could figure out what was going on. She had just dropped off a pack to her boo and didn't want to make the dorm hot if she could avoid it. "Shit! Does anybody else need medical attention?" She asked skeptically as Ramello slipped past her into the sallyport.

"Nah, just him," Jihad said.

Sierra closed the door, locking it instantly. Ramello squinted his eyes from the sunlight and watched as Sierra popped the sallyport gate. He walked out and she escorted him to Medical, glad the walk was deserted besides all the pollen that stained the ground. Their dorm had been the last dorm to get fed lunch and administration had cleared the walk afterwards. "You wanna tell me what happened? Do I need to call a code, sir?" Sierra asked as she knocked on the Medical door.

"Nah, I'm straight. I cut myself on accident." Ramello took a deep breath. The pain in his leg was beginning to get to him. The feeling of the thick and sticky blood and the burning sensation from being cut seemed to be getting more intense the longer that it was exposed to air, and the more he walked. He was gripping his leg, applying pressure at the top to slow the bleeding.

They watched through the glass as Dominique approached, and when she snatched the door open Sierra made a noise, but said nothing. Dominique's eyes widened for a moment before she stepped forward to grab Ramello by the arm and help him into a backroom.

"Oh my, help me get him on the table." Dominique ushered him over to the medical table.

Closing the door, Sierra and Dominique carefully helped Ramello lie on the medical table. "Hand me those scissors over there," Dominique pointed to a pair that was on the table behind her. "What's your name, sir?"

"Dixon..." Ramello seemed calm as he lay on the table. He was in pain and in slight disbelief as he processed what happened to him. He didn't know how he got stabbed. He hadn't even expected the dirty nigga to have been strapped, but it had happened nevertheless. He wished he had known that he was hit before he was pulled off of him or he would have fucked the nigga up even more. He was thankful that he hadn't because he probably would have killed the nigga.

"Hi, Dixon. I'm Nurse Dominique. I'm gonna have to cut these pants off of you, okay?" Her voice was calm and soft as she spoke.

Ramello looked up and met the prettiest, brown, almond-shaped eyes. He couldn't remember the last time that he had been in such close proximity to a woman. Seven years, he had been behind the wall, and three years had gone by since he had a visit from a woman as well. The nurse's kind eyes were unexpectedly comforting to him. "Aiight..." He said and watched as the pretty woman took the scissors from Sierra and began to cut from the bottom of his left pants leg, all the way up to the waistband, and then flipped the material open so she could free his leg.

Cling!

"Oop!" they all looked at the floor to see Ramello's knife had fallen from his waistline.

"I'll get that." Sierra squatted, picked it up, and put it in her pocket.

Dominique shook it off and focused her attention back on his leg.

"Goddamn!" Sierra gasped when she saw the large gash, seeping blood.

Dominique looked back at her friend and gave her a nasty look.

"My bad." She threw her hands up.

"Go grab him a cup of water." The nurse said as she shook her head.

Ramello got a good look at her when she turned around to grab a large blue rubber band, gauze, anti-septic, a needle, and a bottle of some kind of medication. Even though he was lying on the table with a serious injury, he couldn't help but notice how attractive the nurse was. She was thick as hell and curvy, just how he preferred. It was also a plus that she was extremely pretty in the face. Her hair was straight and pulled into a low ponytail at the back of her head and she looked damn good in her powder blue scrubs. He couldn't help but notice that her ass was nice, round, and enticing to him.

Ramello forced himself to look away, his mind immediately going to the gutter. The nurse turned around as she put a pair of blue nitrile gloves on, and then grabbed the rubber band. "Alright, Dixon, this is going to be a bit uncomfortable, but I need to stop this bleeding so we can get this stitched up, okay? It's gonna be tight..." She said as she carefully lifted his thigh, slipped the band beneath it, and tied it above the area where the cut was.

Just as I'm sure that pussy is, Ramello thought. His face twisted at the pinch that came from the tightness of the band.

"Are you feeling light-headed at all?" Dominique looked at Sierra who was handing her a paper cup filled with cool water. "Grab me a straw, please."

Sierra grabbed a bendy straw from a cup near the water

jug, handed it to her, and watched Dominique carefully put the straw in the cup before putting it to Ramello's lips.

He shook his head in response and wrapped his big lips around the straw, quickly sucking down the cool water. The entire time he drank the water, the two locked eyes, unintentionally holding one another's gaze. Sierra watched them, a small smirk pulling at her lips. She knew her friend was a relatively shy woman, eye contact was something that wasn't big on her list, especially not with a stranger. Yet, there she was making googley eyes with an inmate. How she was seeing, it was only going to be a matter of time before she would change her tune. All it was going to take was the right one.

Ramello finished the water and Dominique put the cup down, grabbed pieces of gauze, pressed them to the open wound, and wiped down the areas around it.

"Ssss!" Ramello flinched at her touch.

"Sorry," she said. "Just bear with me a little longer and I will give you something to numb the pain while I stitch you up, okay?"

Staring up at the ceiling, Ramello nodded and took a deep breath to mask his pain. The longer he sat there, the more pain he felt. His mind was reeling as the nurse worked on his leg. Her touch was light, soft, and experienced, as she grabbed a small bucket with warm water, anti-septic soap, and a small wash cloth and cleaned the blood from his leg.

Unexpectedly he felt his dick begin to harden as she cleaned him. Her soft touch along with the warmth of the water and her kind demeanor had him rising, unable to hide the growing bulge in what was left of his pants. A part of him felt embarrassed that he was reacting that way in response to being cared for, but at the same time, how could he not? He was in a room with two good-looking women who were hovering over him, touching him, and essentially catering to his needs.

Looking away from the ceiling, he looked at the female officer who was still in the room with them and found her staring straight at the growing tent in his pants. She was biting her lip, staring unabashedly. He felt his skin grow hot and his dick only grew stiffer, throbbing with desire as images of both the good-looking women with their pretty, full lips wrapped around the shaft of his dick flooded his mind.

The nurse cleared her throat and her eyes flickered up to Sierra. "Thanks, Ms. Jones. That's all I needed." She dismissed the woman.

Sierra pursed her lips and narrowed her eyes at her but said nothing and moved toward the door. "Oh, okay. You want him for yourself, I get it. I'll get out of your hair."

Dominique looked up at her with a glare, annoyed that she was putting her friend out like that. She was pushing the whole fucking with an inmate thing like she hadn't already told her that she wasn't willing to risk her license. She just couldn't have her friend in there making the man uncomfortable by staring at his dick. It was unprofessional and quite frankly, awkward. She rolled her eyes when Sierra flipped her the bird before slipping out of the door.

"Sorry about that." She mumbled before resuming her cleanup of the man's leg.

"It's all good." Ramello's voice was deep and his eyes were low with desire. He was enjoying being handled with care by the attractive nurse and now that they were alone, he felt more comfortable getting in his mode. There was something about the way that she was looking into his eyes that let him know that if he was to shoot his shot, that she just might pick up what he was putting down. "Sorry about *that.*" He looked pointedly at the large tent in his pants.

The sweet giggle that left her pretty pink lips was everything he needed to hear and didn't even know it. "It's natural. Nothing I'm not used to." A small smile pulled at her lips as she picked up a needle and began loading it with medicine.

"Yeah... I'm sure you are used to makin' niggas hard and shit." Now more relaxed, he put his hands behind his head and watched her intently as she continued patching him up. The throbbing of his dick had him completely distracted from the pain in his leg. It had begun to go numb anyway from the rubber band slowing the circulation.

Dominique giggled again and positioned herself over his leg so that she could inject him with a numbing anesthesia so she could stitch his leg back up. "I think you're just saying that." She couldn't help but glance at the tent again, his length was straining against the fabric. It looked big and her mind immediately began to wonder what it *really* looked like. "That's just your adrenaline pumping." She tried to come up with an excuse to keep her from feeling flattered.

"Mmm, maybe..." Romello licked his lips and smirked as he watched her turn to grab more gauze and noticed the wave of her hand as she fanned herself. She was just as hot and bothered as he was. "I think it's cause how good you're taking care of me."

She laughed as she turned back to him. "You're funny. You have a habit of flirting with every nurse you come in contact with?" She looked over her shoulder at him.

"Only the pretty ones." He gave her a boyish grin, showing off a nice set of white teeth.

She waved him off, and turned back around, chuckling and reminding herself that he was an inmate. She was used to being flirted with when it came to patients, whether it was in the jail, or at her second job at the hospital. It came with the job, but it was rare that she entertained the flirting. For some reason, though, she found herself entertaining Ramello and his antics. It was so natural, she couldn't stop herself and that threw her for a loop a bit.

"Alright, let me numb you up a little bit so we can sew you up and get you outta here."

"Damn, you tryna get rid of me already?" Ramello teased.

"You want to bleed out?" She bent over his leg and injected him with the anesthetic.

"Aiight, I get your point." He chuckled then went quiet and allowed the nurse to do what she needed to do.

"Okay," she pulled the rubber band loose and then grabbed her needle and surgical thread. "Big pinch, take a deep breath... Good."

Ramello's face was stoic as Dominique gracefully and fairly quickly stitched him up. He didn't feel too much, only the slight tugging that came from the thread as she weaved it through his skin. The cut stretched across nearly the entire diameter of his thigh. He would be feeling that for a few weeks.

"And done." Dominique smiled down at her handiwork and gently rubbed Melly's lower thigh. "How are you feeling?"

"I've been worse." He shrugged and sat up on his elbows. "Thank you." He licked his lips, his eyes on her plump ass as she walked over to a cupboard and opened it where she grabbed an extra pair of pants and boxers. He wanted like hell to just be able to rub on the woman's phat booty, but he knew that was just the caged-up dog in him that was feeling the urge to mate.

"Of course," she smiled at him and met his eyes, approaching him with the clothing. She cleared her throat when she was back at his side. "You need help getting out the rest of those clothes and into these new ones?"

"If it's not too much to ask."

Dominique swallowed hard, her heart speeding up in her

chest. Of course, he was going to need her help after his injury, and he was also going to have to linger in the office for a bit until the numbing in his leg went away, even if it was in the infirmary part of Medical. She couldn't risk him walking around in the dorm and having him collapse because his thigh was numb. So, he would be spending a little bit of time with her that day. "No problem. Here, let me cut the other side off for you so we don't have to make you lift so much." She suggested and grabbed the scissors and cut the other side of his pants off of him from the pants leg up, and did the same with the boxers.

Her eyes nearly bulged out of her head when she removed the fabric from his nether regions. As soon as she exposed the bottom half of his body, Ramello's thick, hard dick went springing up landing against his bellybutton with an audible smack.

"Damn..."

A smug smirk was on Ramello's face as he watched the nurse eye his veiny dick with a look of awe on her face. His day had started rough. The last place he had expected himself to be was in the nurse's office because a fuck nigga had tried him. All the same, he liked the turn of events that his day had taken. He may have been injured, but he could tell the experience that came with the nurse who was caring for him was going to be worth it.

Nurse Dominique was looking and interested. He had a chance, and that's all he needed to know. If she was willing to go that far, he wanted to see just *how* far he could get her to go.

He watched her blink a few times before snatching her eyes away from his length. She turned to grab the bucket, a soiled washcloth that she used to clean blood from his thigh and dumped them in the sink. Ramello grabbed his dick in his hand and slowly began stroking it to her physique. The worst she could do was tell him to stop and put it away, or tell the officer to write him a Disciplinary Report for a B-11.

And Ms. Jones ain't gone be wit' that shit, anyways. His teeth were lodged into his bottom lip, the head of his dick leaking pre-cum in anticipation of her reaction to him stroking himself to her. It was a test to see how she would react.

Dominique turned around with fresh water and a clean washcloth and paused, heat lighting up her eyes when she saw him fisting his erection. She bit her lip, shook her head slightly, and chuckled before walking back to his side. "You're trouble, aren't you, Dixon?"

"I may be." His voice was low and thick with lust, thoroughly enjoying the direction that their interaction was going. He liked that she hadn't gotten offended and hadn't told him to stop. He continued pleasuring himself as she dunked the cloth into the soapy water and then rung it out over his thighs and pelvis. His eyes fluttered at the warmth of the water, and then the nurse's soft touch as she scrubbed the blood that remained on the rest of the skin that had trickled down his legs and over his pelvis.

"Hmmm..." she curiously met his eyes.

"Do you like trouble, Nurse Dominique?"

"I try to avoid trouble as much as possible." Her eyes drifted back down to Ramello's dick in his hand. "It usually has a way of finding me, though..."

Ramello grunted softly. "Trouble's good sometimes. It can be *fun*." He increased the speed of his strokes.

"That may be true, but it also comes with consequences." She met his eyes again to let him know that she was serious. Still, she continued washing his lower half, cleaning both of his legs and around his pelvis, avoiding his dick and the base of his shaft, the places she wanted to touch the most, but was fighting hard against the urge to do so.

"Only if you get caught." He was enticing her. Ramello stopped his stroking and held his dick by the base of his shaft and waved it at her.

Dominique found Ramello to be extremely attractive. He was tall, in shape by what she could tell from the two defined abs that peeked from underneath his shirt, and by how toned his legs were. His dick was the definition of edible, like her favorite Snicker's bar and she couldn't help the dirty way she was imagining slurping him up for her own pleasure. The fact that she wasn't supposed to even be watching him pleasure himself, and then asking her to participate had her clit thumping against the seat of her panties.

Wordlessly, Dominique dipped the cloth back into the soapy water, rug it out a bit, then with it still in hand she wrapped it around Ramello's dick and slowly cleaned it for him.

Ramello inhaled sharply, his excitement growing when she gave in and *touched* him. "Damn..." His eyes shut and he dropped his head back in pleasure. Again, the touch was soft as she massaged his length with the cloth barrier, but it still felt good because it was a touch other than *his*. It had been seven long years since he had an intimate touch from a woman, so the moment that he was having with the nurse was everything that he needed and more.

"You like that?" Her voice was low and seductive as she watched the pleasure play out on his face.

"Hell yeah," he groaned. His hips were thrusting against her hand.

Dominique removed the towel, gripped Ramello's dick in both her hands, and began jacking it with her soapy, gloved hands, twisting them in opposite directions. Her grip was firm, yet soft at the same time, her small hands expertly massaging his girth.

"Ugh!" He groaned again when she stilled one hand, gripping the base of his shaft, focusing her attention on the head with short, controlled strokes. Pressure was building in his core as he felt himself about to cum.

It had only been a few minutes that she was stroking his length for him, but he was so worked up with excitement that he was struggling to prolong the moment like he so desperately wanted to.

"Cum for me, Dixon." She cooed to him.

"Fuuuuck." His entire body shook as his dick erupted, sending spurt after spurt of cum shooting every which way. He had never cum so hard in his life. "Goddamn..." He was breathless when he spoke.

"Mhmm... let it allll out." A satisfied grin was on her face, and her pretty almond-shaped eyes almost looked closed as she looked down at him. Once she was sure that she had milked him of every drop he had, Dominique let go of his shaft, grabbed the bucket and washcloth again, and began cleaning up the mess that her patient had made.

"Shit, girl... I needed that." Ramello shook his head in disbelief and laughed. He almost felt like he was in a dream and was waiting for himself to wake up, but it was very much his reality.

"I'm sure you did." Dominique giggled as she bent over to clean up the drops of cum that had landed on the floor around the medical table.

Ramello lazily turned and looked at Dominique with hooded, lust-filled eyes. "You know you just fucked up, right?"

For a few moments she didn't reply, just continued cleaning. "Yeah, I knew you were trouble..." She shook her head at herself.

"As long as you know."

Available Now On All Platforms

OTHER BOOKS BY

<u>URBAN AINT DEAD</u>

Tales 4rm Da Dale

The Hottest Summer Ever

Hittin' Licks For The Holidays: Atlanta

Wet Dreams On Lockdown: The Nurse

By **Elijah R. Freeman**

Despite The Odds

By **Juhnell Morgan**

Good Girl Gone Rogue

By **Manny Black**

Hittaz

Hittaz 2

Hittaz 3

Hittaz 4

Coldhearted

By **Lou Garden Price, Sr.**

Charge It To The Game

Charge It To The Game 2

A Summer To Remember With My Hitta

Snatched Up By A Hitta

Santa Sent Me A Real One For Christmas

Wet Dreams on Lockdown: The Unit Manager

By **Nai**

A Setup For Revenge

By **Ashley Williams**

Ridin' For You

Trickin' on a Heaux for Christmas: A BBW Love Story

Homie Hoppin' For The Holidays

By **Telia Teanna**

The State's Witness

The State's Witness 2

The State's Witness 3

By **Kyiris Ashley**

Stuck In The Trenches

Stuck In The Trenches 2

By **Huff Tha Great**

The Swipe

By **Toōla**

Melted the Heart of a Menace

By P. Wise

Merry Trapmas: Ice & Frost

By **Mia Sky**

Thug Me The Right Way

By **DiamondATL & Nai**

<u>**Coming Soon From**</u>
URBAN AINT DEAD

The Hottest Summer Ever 2
THE G-CODE
How To Publish A Book From Prison
Tales 4rm Da Dale 2
By **Elijah R. Freeman**

Hittaz 4
Coldhearted 2
By **Lou Garden Price, Sr.**

The Swipe 2
By **Toola**

Good Girl Gone Rogue 2
By **Manny Black**

Despite The Odds 2
Hittin' Licks For The Holidays: Chicago
By **Juhnell Morgan**

Charge It To The Game 3
By **Nai**

Ridin For You, Too
Wet Dreams On Lockdown: The Female C.O
By **Telia Teanna**

A Setup For Revenge 2
By **Ashley Williams**

A Gangsta's Last Kiss
By **Mia Sky**

Pretti & The Beast
Wet Dreams On Lockdown: Lieutenant Grace
By **P. Wise**

Wet Dreams On Lockdown: The Counselor
By **Paris Iman**

Wet Dreams On Lockdown: The Male C.O
By **Tamyra Griffin**

Wet Dreams On Lockdown: The Captain
By **TN Jones**

Wet Dreams On Lockdown: The Warden
By **Shawnice**

BOOKS BY

URBAN AINT DEAD's C.E.O

<u>Elijah R. Freeman</u>

Triggadale

Triggadale 2

Triggadale 3

Tales 4rm Da Dale

The Hottest Summer Ever

Murda Was The Case

Murda Was The Case 2

Murda Was The Case 3

Hittin' Licks For The Holidays: Atlanta

Wet Dreams On Lockdown: The Nurse